About the Author

Taiba Albahrani is a 16-year-old lover of books, writer, and author of the new novel, *A Mysterious Marking*. The young Emirati author writes fiction as well as prose and poetry. She finished writing her first book while still a student in high school and is on her way to writing more.

While balancing between school and writing, Taiba also enjoys spending her time traveling through the pages of a good book and waiting for her Hogwarts letter to arrive. Some of her other favorite pastimes are scrolling through her Twitter feed and binge-watching Netflix.

Dedication

To my loving family.
And all those times you annoyed me while I was writing ♥.
And to all those whose markings will never fade.

Taiba Albahrani

A MYSTERIOUS MARKING

AUSTIN MACAULEY PUBLISHERS™
LONDON • CAMBRIDGE • NEW YORK • SHARJAH

Copyright © Taiba Albahrani (2020)

The right of Taiba Albahrani to be identified as author of this work has been asserted by the author in accordance with Federal Law No. (7) of UAE, Year 2002, Concerning Copyrights and Neighboring Rights.

All rights reserved. No part of this publication may be reproduced, stored in a retrieval system, or transmitted in any form or by any means, electronic, mechanical, photocopying, recording, or otherwise, without the prior permission of the publishers.

Any person who commits any unauthorized act in relation to this publication may be liable to legal prosecution and civil claims for damages.

Austin Macauley is committed to publishing works of quality and integrity. In this spirit, we are proud to offer this book to our readers; however, the story, the experiences, and the words are the author's alone.

The age category suitable for the books' contents has been classified and defined in accordance to the Age Classification System issued by the National Media Council.

ISBN – 9789948347149 – (Paperback)
ISBN – 9789948347156 – (E-Book)

Application Number: MC-10-01-2133308
Age Classification: E

Printer Name: iPrint Global Ltd
Printer Address: Witchford, England

First Published (2020)
AUSTIN MACAULEY PUBLISHERS FZE
Sharjah Publishing City
P.O Box [519201]
Sharjah, UAE
www.austinmacauley.ae
+971 655 95 202

Acknowledgments

First, thank you, the reader, for taking the time and reading my book and thank you to Austin Macauley Publishers for taking a chance on this book and giving it a home.

Thank you to my mother, who has always been the number one supporter of this book and of me. Thank you for staying up 'til seven in the morning with a cup of tea, reading the sloppy earlier drafts of the book and giving me the best advice and encouragement. This book wouldn't have been what it is now if it wasn't for your help. Thank you for believing the impossible and making me believe it too.

Thank you to my father, for always believing in me even when I don't believe in myself. Thank you for always cheering me on to do my very best. Thank you for encouraging and supporting me through everything I do. Trust me when I say that all the incredible things you do for us don't go unnoticed. Thank you for always striving to make us happy.

Thank you to my sisters for staying up for hours, reading the book out loud with me, and sharing the most hilarious (but very helpful) comments about the story. Thank you for being my cheerleaders my whole life. Thank you to my little brother, whom I love more than anything in this world.

Thank you to the coolest aunt in the world (who happens to be mine). Your mere presence in my life means the world to me. Thank you to my favorite cousin Fatima for always being my greatest friend and supporter. You inspire me to never stop chasing my wildest dreams.

Thank you to Haya, for being the super amazing friend that you are and making me soar with all the love and support you always give. Thank you for always believing in me and supporting me every step of the way. Thank you to Mariam M. for always getting super excited with me over it all and giving me the push I needed to do anything.

Thank you to Dalia, for teaching me the meaning of friendship. You speak the same kind of crazy I do. Thank you to Taif, my oldest friend, for always being around. I know our lovely friendship will last. Thank you to Mariam E., for always sprinkling my life with joy. Just seeing you makes me happy. Thank you to Mais, the greatest friend I could ask for. Thank you for simply existing. All the joy and support you give me every day is what keeps me going. Thank you for believing in me and always being there to make sure I knew that. You are irreplaceable.

Thank you to Miss Yasmin, Miss Jessica, and all the great teachers who have given us so much of their time and effort. Your lessons will never be forgotten.

Thank you to the talented illustrator, Sandra Winther, who brought the cover of this book to life in the most beautiful way imaginable. Your hard work and unmatched creativity were essential to make this book whole.

Thank you to Mais Albakri, Matthew Smith, Mohammad Ayoub, the production team, and everyone who has contributed in the journey of this book's publication. I truly appreciate all the time and effort you have put into this project.

CHAPTER ONE

It was quiet. Only the sound of gentle wind and twittering birds could be heard in the dark that was soon to be lit up by the early sun as it came out of its hiding place. A breeze of cold morning air hit the young girl's face and carried her long red hair behind her as she ran back to the big old building. She reached the tall iron gates and pushed them slowly open. Their rusty hinges gave a loud screech that made her flinch. Then she squeezed herself in carefully. After tiptoeing up the stairs and sneaking through the dark halls, Amara found her room and slid inside, careful not to wake anyone. She quietly got out of the old pair of boots and oversized coat she was wearing and crept into bed, pretending to be asleep this whole time.

After about ten minutes, the bells started ringing and it was time for everyone to wake up.

"Wake up! It's time for breakfast!" The girl from the other bed shouted at the sleeping kids in the room.

Amara peeked out from under her blanket. The girl who had just called for them to get up was making her bed. She stretched and gave out a yawn then turned back and started shaking everyone awake. The sun had risen and was casting light around the room from the tiny window in the corner. It was a small room but as many beds as would fit were crammed inside of it.

"Come on, get up!" called the girl one last time as she walked out of the room.

Amara sat up on her bed and gave out a fake yawn while rubbing her eyes. The other sleepy kids also pulled themselves up from under their blankets. The sisters, Tarra and Tanzie, slid out of their shared bunk bed and mummy walked out of the room. Jovie – the sixteen-year-old girl with chocolate brown skin – nudged her brother Sev awake and followed them out. Amara went to wake up her own little brother from the top bunk and they headed to the bathrooms.

"Hurry up, children," called one of the women walking down the hall and ringing the bells, "don't forget to wash up well before getting down for breakfast."

Amara found herself a free bathroom and walked inside to wash her face. She looked at the dirty mirror on the wall. She wiped the glass with her sleeve and stared at her reflection. Amara was a pretty girl. She had a heart-shaped face with an elegant pointed chin, delicate nose, and big ocean blue eyes. But the most unique thing about her was her hair. She had long, striking red hair with thin streaks of orange and yellow between the red. It was straight but turned to waves at the bottom, and it constantly looked like beautiful flames of fire. Amara fixed the uneven short bangs she had cut as to cover the mark between her eyebrows. The strange mark burnt into her flesh.

Everybody had one. At the age of seven, every child in the land of Kumilaka got a marking on their forehead. It slowly started appearing before their seventh birthday arrived, and the day they turned seven years old, it could clearly be seen on their skin and will be forever. The marking you got determined the corral you'd be in and your role in the community. You could be an Educator, Healer, Laborer, Fisher, Hunter, Messenger, Carer, or any of the others. Everyone had a certain corral, a known role in the community. Well, everyone but Amara. When Amara was nearing her seventh year, her marking started to show like every other child. Her family and friends and even she were all trying to guess what her marking was going to be, what corral she'd be in. Was she going to be a Hunter like her father, an Educator like her mother, or something else? But when her seventh year was complete, the marking that appeared on her skin was unknown. No one had seen it before. That meant she didn't fit in any of the corrals. She didn't fit in the community. She had no role.

CHAPTER TWO

The dining hall was as loud and crowded as always. Hungry kids were running down the stairs and filling into the large room to find their places on the long wooden tables where their food will be served. Amara looked through the crowd and found her brother sitting on one of the tables. She headed towards him, putting her hand inside her pocket to check for something.

"Morning," Amara said as she sat down across from her brother. She smiled at the little boy with spikes of green hair like grass growing on his head. Neo had wide-set eyes the color of chestnut that stood out on his beautiful, freckled round face. His arms and legs, however, were looking a bit thin.

"Morning," he said, smiling.

"Good morning," said Sev, the boy who shared the bunk bed with Neo. He was older than him, twelve years old, and had the same chocolate brown skin as his older sister. His silver hair was growing into an afro. "Am I the only one who's starving?" he held tight to his stomach and fell onto the table dramatically.

"You are always starving," Amara said and rolled her eyes.

"I strongly agree," his sister Jovie said as she slid into the empty seat next to Amara.

"The food is here!" Neo said eagerly. Just as he said it, one of the Carers – a nice young woman with pink hair – came to their table with a tray in her hands. She passed the plates and spoons down the table and then scooped something from the big bowl on the tray into each of their plates.

"Not oatmeal again," groaned Sev.

The lady with pink hair smiled at him. "I don't like it either," she whispered. "But I heard one of the Carers say they might be serving chicken for lunch next week."

"For real?" Sev said, and Amara could see the excitement in his face.

The young Carer smiled again and gave him a wink. Then she walked on to the other table.

"Chicken!" Neo said, his eyes widening.

"Oh, I can't wait." Sev licked his lips.

"Yeah, well," Jovie said as she stirred her oatmeal with a spoon, "right now, you're stuck with this."

Sev stared down at his own oatmeal and frowned.

"You better eat it all up." The girl who woke them up this morning was standing at the foot of the table. "It's not right to throw away perfectly good food." She sat down next to Amara. Coreen had very orange hair that she always wore in pigtails and a very smug face too. She was a Carer in training and for some reason that made her think that she had the right to boss them all around like she was in charge or something. And she always acted like she knew everything, which very much annoyed Amara. "It's been hard for the Carers to provide much food for the children lately because money hasn't been that well. So, you should be thankful you have anything to eat at all."

"I don't see you gulping down that oatmeal," said Jovie.

Coreen put a spoonful of the nasty brown substance in her mouth and swallowed. Jovie rolled her eyes.

"It's also very good for you," Coreen continued. She started blabbering on about the benefits of oatmeal and Amara felt like plugging her ears shut. She took a bite out of her own plate. It wasn't that good but she was really hungry so she didn't really care. She looked at Neo. He had already finished his plate and was wiping the edges clean, trying to get more of it. She pushed her plate toward him. He looked up.

"You have it, I'm not that hungry," she said to him. He shook his head. "Seriously, I'm not hungry," she repeated, but it wasn't very convincing, because as she was saying that, her stomach gave a loud and meaningful growl. Neo pushed the plate back toward her.

"Come on, please? I'm going to Elianah's today and I'm grabbing a bite with her, okay?" she placed the plate in front of him. "Now, eat your breakfast. I have a surprise for you when you're finished," she whispered.

"A surprise? What is it?" he asked excitedly.

"Shhh," she placed her finger on her lips. "I'll tell you after you finish your plate."

He looked at her for a moment, clearly trying to decide if she was telling the truth, and then nodded his head slowly and ate the oatmeal.

Chapter Three

Amara was fourteen years old. Her brother Neo was six, and turning seven soon. She loved her little brother more than anything, and did everything she could to take care of him. She wasn't really supposed to be taking care of him – considering she was only a kid herself – but she didn't have a choice. Their mother died six years ago after giving birth to him. Their father left one year after that, leaving his children in his sister's care. Two-and-a-half years later, Aunt Kaila died in an accident, leaving eleven-year-old Amara all alone to take care of her little brother when she could barely take care of herself.

Since they were orphaned children with no family left, they were brought here to be looked after by the Carers. Usually, the girls and boys were separated into different rooms, but siblings could request staying together. Amara didn't want to let Neo out of her sight, and so they were both assigned the same room. This place was where all the children with no parents or families, or with families that couldn't care for them, came. It wasn't exactly an orphanage though. Yes, they provided food and a place to sleep for all those kids, but they still gave them the freedom to do pretty much whatever they wanted. As long as they went to school and corral training, made it back by eight, and stayed out of trouble, the Carers didn't mind. The place was called The Children's Home. Amara didn't see it as a home though. She had a home. Even though the house where she used to live with her mother and father was locked and they weren't exactly allowed to go inside, she dreamed of the day she might be able to live in her childhood home again. It was a small house right at the edge of the forest. They had locked it after Amara's dad had left

Kumilaka. But that didn't stop Amara from sneaking in through the broken window every once in a while to retrieve some of their old belongings or sometimes just stare at the rooms she grew up in. That's what she did this morning. She woke up very early and snuck out of bed to go to her old house and get something. She was careful to make it back before sunrise because the Carers won't be too happy if they knew she'd left the home after curfew and also broken the rules by trespassing, not that it had stopped her before. Not to mention, Coreen will not get off her back if she found out.

Breakfast was almost over and Coreen got up to help some of the Carers gather the dirty dishes. So, Amara took the chance.

"Neo," she whispered to her brother who sat in front of her, "under the table," she took something out of her pocket and held it out for him under the dining room table. He reached out to grab it and then held it in his lap. His eyes widened in surprise.

"Crayons?" he whispered back excitedly, "where did you find these?"

Neo was always really into drawing. He wasn't that bad for a six-year-old. A while ago, Elianah – Amara's best friend – gave him a small notebook with blank pages, and he drew in it ever since. Just last week, he was saying how nice it would be to have something to color his drawings with.

"I went to our old house," she whispered back, glancing around to make sure Coreen wasn't in earshot. "I found them in a box under my bed where I hid some of my things from you."

He smiled wide. "Thanks."

"No problem," she smiled back. "Now, go get ready for school so you can color when you get back."

Chapter Four

The land of Kumilaka was a happy and peaceful society. When there was a conflict or a problem, a meeting was held. All the people of Kumilaka stated their opinion and voted to what they saw fit as the best solution to that problem. The Advisors were the corral in charge of making the final decision. They gathered up all the votes and announced the decision that had been made. After Amara got her strange marking, a meeting was called.

"We are here today to discuss the future of Child Amara," said Advisor Bevanios. He was an old man and was almost bald, except for the small patches of white left on his head. He called her Child Amara. There were no middle names or family names in Kumilaka. Everyone was called by their corral followed by their first and only name. Children that still hadn't received their markings were called Child. Of course, Amara did receive her marking, but since she didn't fit into any of the corrals, she was still referred to as Child.

"As you all may know," continued Advisor Bevanios, "Amara has completed her seventh year and received her marking. The marking, however, is not of a familiar corral, and that is quite peculiar." He said the last thing in a low voice and glanced at Amara as he did so. He looked at her for just a moment with curious eyes and then turned back to the people.

"Is it one of the old markings?" asked one of the people in the front row.

"Is it a warrior marking?" said another.

"Are we going into war?!" someone yelled.

That started a buzz of nervous talking. There were also many glances at Amara sitting in the front row. Little Amara sat back in her seat and tried to make herself as small as possible. Her father tightened his grip around her shoulders as if to say, "Don't worry, I'm here."

"Silence, please," said Advisor Bevanios in his booming voice. The room quieted down and everyone looked at the old man in anticipation. "We do not know what her marking means," he continued calmly, "no, it is not one we have seen in the past. No, it is not one of the three ancient corrals' markings. It is the first time in the history of Kumilaka that a new and unknown marking has appeared. It is the first time that a marking that doesn't belong to a corral has appeared. Now, we must discuss what is to happen to the child bearing this unusual marking."

The debate started. The community didn't know what to do with her. She couldn't continue going to school because children go to school only from the age of three to the end of their sixth year. After getting their marking, they start training and working with their corral, but since Amara didn't have a corral, she didn't have anywhere to go.

Her father offered to take her along with him on his hunting trips and train her to be a part of the Hunters' corral. The community agreed to give this a try. But it was clear after the first week of training that Amara wasn't at all fit for being a Hunter. She cried when an animal was killed and vomited at the sight of the dead bloody creatures. At the end, it was decided that she was to help around the community and do simple jobs or errands for all the different corrals, and get some training while doing so. She was to do this until she reached her sixteenth year. That is when her corral will be decided. She would have tried all the different corrals and been observed in each one. So, the Advisors will choose the corral they saw her most fit to, the one she will continue to train and work in for the rest of her life. Of course, even if they did choose the corral she was most suited for, she would still not be as perfect in that corral as everyone else was in theirs. Amara also took some extra tasks in her free time. She asked to help around and run errands for the different corrals and they paid her some money for the jobs she did. She used the extra money to buy things for herself and Neo when they needed them. More food or other stuff the Carers couldn't provide.

Today, she was scheduled to help the Messengers deliver supplies from the market to the Healers. There were a lot of boxes and a lot of Healers, and carrying heavy loads was not Amara's favorite thing in the world. She wasn't very suited for the job either, with her weak and muscle-less legs and arms. Her last stop was at her best friend Elianah's house. She put the giant wooden box on the floor and sighed with pain. Wiping the sweat off her forehead, she knocked on the door. The door opened and out came Amara's best friend, the most beautiful girl she'd ever met. She had the softest features and rosiest cheeks, her big and pretty baby blue curls bounced around her. Her beautiful sparkling eyes had long blue lashes. She had high and wide cheekbones, full pink lips, and a lingering wide smile. Standing there, beautiful and cheerful as always, was Elianah. On her forehead, right in the middle between the two high arching blue brows that gave her a look of slight surprise and continuous interest, was a clear and delicate marking, the marking of a Healer.

"Mara!" she said excitedly and jumped out to hug her friend. Her blue curls tickled Amara's cheeks as she held her into a hug. "I haven't seen you all week! That is so not okay," she scolded.

"I'm sorry. It was just a very busy week. Hunter Burk and Educator Merla are getting married soon. So, I had to deliver messages all over Kumilaka," Amara said, heaving a sigh.

"Oh yeah, I've heard, how lovely!" Then Elianah took another look at Amara and frowned. "You look pale, Mara! Have you eaten breakfast? Don't tell me you've been carrying these heavy boxes all day with an empty stomach! How many times have I told you? Breakfast is the most important meal of the day. They don't just say that, it's true!" She moved Amara aside, carried the box sitting by the door, and walked into her house.

"What are you doing, Eli? Give me that!" Amara followed and tried to take the box away from Elianah but was unsuccessful.

"Don't be silly, you delivered it and now your job is done. I'm going to take it down to Nana Eve and you help yourself to the blueberry muffins on the counter. When I'm back, I better find the plate half-empty. I mean it!" she called as she walked down the hall.

CHAPTER FIVE

Amara sat down on the stool by the counter. She looked at the plate with the delicious looking muffins and her stomach gave a loud rumble of hunger. Then she felt something furry brush against her knees. She looked down and saw Asha, Elianah's pet cat. She was a Siberian cat that they rescued four years ago. She was a giant furball really, the color of smoke gray, her eyes were a piercing green. Amara stroked the top of the cat's head and smiled at the feel of the soft hair between her fingers. She scratched under the cat's ears, like she knew she liked, and Asha purred in pleasure. After a few minutes of enjoyable petting, Asha walked away to her bowl of food.

Amara looked at the plate of muffins again. The heavenly smell of freshly baked muffins filled her nostrils. She sighed and slowly picked one up. Elianah will make her eat them anyway so she might as well give in to the hunger. She took a bite and the delightful moist and fruity taste of the flavorful muffin filled her mouth with joy! This was definitely one of Elianah's mother's muffins. She was a Baker, and she made the most delicious baked goods that Amara had ever tasted. But Elianah was a Healer like her grandmother. Anyone who'd met her would know she was perfect for that corral. She had such a kind and caring heart. She was gentle but strict at the same time when it came to her patient's health. She would know if you were sick or if there was anything wrong with you just by looking at your face. She was also Amara's best friend. They were friends since childhood. Way before she got her strange marking and some of the kids started making fun of her and making up stories behind her back. Before Amara started being distant and shutting people out after her mother's death and father's abandonment. Even then, Elianah still kept close to Amara. She didn't care that Amara didn't want to talk to anyone or wanted to be left alone. She knew that deep down Amara really wanted a friend. Someone to stick around no matter what and she was that someone.

"Sorry I took so long," Elianah said, walking into the kitchen, her blue curls bouncing behind her, "Nana Eve needed my help with a patient," she poured herself a glass of water. "You remember little Zuri? Lavinia's sister? She got into a fight with that boy Brodick from down the street about whose sister caught a bigger fish or something!" She gulped down the water, "Brodick got sent home in a bad shape, that girl's got some strength in her for a five-year-old!"

"Urghh… I bet she does!" Amara groaned, "If she's anything like that wicked sister of hers, then she's an awful child!"

"Oh, not *that* again, you and Lavinia have always hated each other and for no good reason at all!"

"No, no, no. I didn't always hate Lavinia. She hated me first, remember? When we were six, she pushed me down the stairs! Then she pretended it was an accident, and when no one was looking, she laughed and told me to go cry to my daddy! After that, she continued to be mean to me and I've hated her ever since. But she's the one who started it, not me."

"Oh yeah, I remember when you fell, you poor thing."

Amara smiled; glad to have Elianah back on her side. Then she looked at her watch and stood up.

"Speaking of dear old Lavinia," she said, "my shift at the Fishing corral starts in twenty minutes. I better get going. I really hope I don't see her there," she rolled her eyes.

"Do you have to go?" Elianah said, getting up too. "You just got here. I barely got the chance to see you. Can't you stay just for a little while longer?" she pleaded.

"You know I can't, Eli. I have to go. I'll try and find some time to swing by, okay?"

"You promise?"

"I'll try."

"I miss you, Mara. You train and work all the time. It's not good for you. You have to get some rest. Drop some of your extra shifts," Elianah said. Her voice was concerned. She paused, "Mara, I had that feeling again," she mumbled.

Amara sighed. "What feeling?" she said. Even though she knew perfectly well what Elianah meant.

"That bad feeling," Elianah explained, nonetheless. "The feeling I have before something bad happens," she spoke in a low voice, like she was afraid someone would hear her. "Remember when I had it at school, and Laureen broke her arm? Or when I had it two years ago and Nana Eve got a stroke?" she shuddered a little.

"You're being paranoid. It's probably nothing." She looked her in the eye. "I'm fine, Eli. I can take it, I really can."

"You shouldn't though."

She glanced at her watch again. "I'm gonna be late," she looked back up at her friend. "Don't worry about me. I'm just fine."

Elianah nodded slowly. Then she ran to the kitchen and brought back another one of the blueberry muffins wrapped in a napkin. "For the way there." She smiled and handed it to her. Amara smiled back at her.

"Thank you. See you soon," she said.

"See you soon."

CHAPTER SIX

Amara walked down to the seaside where the Fishing corral was. She rarely took any extra shifts here, because it did require a lot of knowledge to work in the Fisher corral, knowledge she didn't have. She spotted Fisher Eaton, who she recognized as someone sort of in charge. She walked over to him.

"Good morning, Fisher Eaton," she said politely.

"Good morning," he said, not looking up from his clipboard. He scrawled one last thing on his papers and then looked up and saw Amara. "Oh hello," he said, like he had just noticed her, "how can I help you, my dear?"

"Um—I—I'm supposed to come and help around here today," she said hesitantly.

"You're supposed to—?" he started to ask, confused.

"My name is Amara," she said, hoping that might help.

Recognition crossed over his face. He looked back at his clipboard and flipped through the pages, looking for something. "Ah, yes. Your volunteering shift is today. You are right on time," he said approvingly.

She waited a few seconds before asking, "So, how can I help?"

"Oh yes, how can you help?" He looked around him. "How can you help?" he mumbled, more to himself than to Amara. Amara looked down at her shoes. She knew they didn't really need her here. There were enough trained Fishers here, everyone had their own job and everyone knew what to do. Even if they did need more help, she wasn't any use to them. She wasn't really a part of the Fishing corral. So, she hadn't received the proper training that qualified her to work here like all the other kids who had got their Fisher marking at seven.

"Yes!" Fisher Eaton said suddenly, "I remembered that we really need someone to help in cleaning the fishing boats. They're extremely dirty and haven't been properly washed in forever."

Amara knew he had just made that up but she went along with it anyway. "Yeah, sure, I'll be glad to help with it."

"Great," he said, smiling. He was clearly glad she was cooperating, and Amara felt like he wanted to get rid of her as soon as possible so he could get back to his work. "Let me just show you the way now," she followed him as he headed to where a couple of boats sat on the beach. "We'll get you some supplies and you can get started."

"Okay."

"Eaton!" someone called from a few feet away, "we need you back there."

"I'm coming," Fisher Eaton called back. He turned to Amara. "You going to be okay?" he asked.

"Uh—yeah."

"Eaton, hurry up, will you?!" the same guy shouted.

"I'm coming, Zen!" he called to him. "I have to go," he said distractedly to Amara, he looked down at his clipboard and scribbled something on it. He turned to go but then looked back at Amara. "Oh, I almost forgot. Hey, Lavinia, would you come and help her, please? She needs some cleaning supplies to wash the boats." He was talking to a girl who had just walked by with an empty fishing net in her hands. "Thanks," then he hurried away to meet the other guy.

Amara stood there, not believing how very unlucky she was. A tall and thin girl with short and straight navy blue hair swept to one side stood there in front of her. She had a pale tone of skin. Her eyes were narrow and deep-set and almost pitch black. Her nose was small and pinched. Her lips were thin and pursed as always and had a sly smile playing on them. She had dark thin brows and between them was a marking that said she was a Fisher: Lavinia.

"Well, hello," Lavinia said a moment later. Her voice was rough and had a tone of amusement in it. "I haven't seen you in a while. But I suppose my luck can't last forever, now can it? You had to show your freckly face eventually. So, what are you doing here? Cleaning our boats, huh?" she asked with a smile in her voice.

Amara clenched her fists but said nothing.

"What's wrong? Don't you like your new job? I actually think washing boats is a pretty good promotion from your previous job," she said in mock thoughtfulness, "what was it? Cleaning toilets?"

Amara bit the inside of her cheek to stop herself from saying anything. She was here to work. She needed the extra pay. Lavinia was not going to mess this up for her. "Just give me the supplies and get lost, will you?" she said, trying and failing to control the rising anger in her voice.

"Ohhh, redhead is getting mad, is she?" Lavinia said with a smirk. "Okay, I'll give you what you need to get to work. But you better make those boats spotless." She walked away and came back minutes later with a bucket of water and a sponge. "Now get to work, flame-head," she said and gave Amara a look of disdain. Amara held out her arms to take the bucket. Lavinia looked at her for a moment before handing her the bucket, that's when she pretended to trip and poured the entire bucket of water onto Amara. A sudden rush of freezing cold water splashed onto her skin and her whole body shuddered as the water ran down her shoulders. She still had her hands held out and her mouth was open in shock. She stood there completely frozen in place, yet shivered from head to toe.

"Oops," Lavinia said. She dropped the bucket on the floor and threw the sponge aside. "I guess you'll have to refill it again." She shrugged carelessly. But she didn't leave; she stood there in front of Amara a moment longer, not breaking her gaze. Her eyes were determined and challenging and full of something else. Hate. She finally turned and walked away, leaving Amara, who was still standing in the same position, unable to move.

A few moments later, Amara rubbed her cold hands together, and shook her head to try and hold back the tears from falling. She was not going to cry; she was not going to give Lavinia that satisfaction. She blinked back the tears of anger and humiliation. Her body was shaking as the cold drops of water trickled down her spine. But she was glad that the late morning sun was still up or she would've been really freezing right now. Amara took the empty bucket off the floor and went to fill it up, hoping the hot sun would dry her up soon.

CHAPTER SEVEN

"You can pick up Educator Mila's delivery from the market and then you'll be done for the day," Messenger Antonio – a young man in his twenties who worked with her on her shifts here – told her after checking their schedule. It was the afternoon now and Amara was working on her last shift for the day, back to helping the Messenger corral.

Amara walked down to the market. The place was crowded – as it always was this time of day – with mothers buying things for dinner, fathers buying toys for their kids, men and women selling their goods, and a bunch of other people doing whatever people came to do in the market. It was filled with booths and tables and small shops. Some people even sat on the floor and spread their products on the ground in front of them. The buzz of a hundred chattering people and occasional shouts and calls filled the air. The place was vibrant with colors: fruits and vegetables, herbs and spices, colorful clothes, sparkling jewelry, ancient books, and a million other things. Everywhere you looked, there was something that caught your eye. You couldn't help but get lured into one of the many booths where a seller stood convincing you that you can't live without their product and that you need to buy it immediately.

Amara squeezed herself between shoulders and slid between the swarms of people. She couldn't help but imagine that familiar scent of smoke that had filled her nostrils as her heart tightened in her chest with fear, the one that always came when she found herself in the market. She pushed the awful memory from her head. Amara reached the shop she was supposed to pick the delivery up from. She took the two bags from the man working there and left the market.

She walked to the place she was supposed to meet the other Messenger and put down the heavy bags of fruit on one of the abandoned boxes on the floor and sat down on another. Doran, the other Messenger, was supposed to meet her here two minutes ago to pick them up and take them to Educator Mila's home. Her shift was supposed to end now so she could pick up Neo from school. But Doran was nowhere to be seen. She looked at her old, battered watch.

Six minutes passed…then ten… Where was he? Doran was a young boy, not much older than she was actually. She worked with him on many of her shifts in the Messenger corral, which was the corral she worked in the most since it didn't need that much experience or skill. But that didn't mean it was an easy job either, it required strength and speed. Amara didn't think she had any of those things. Doran however, had both. He was a tall boy with long limbs and had excellent speed. Amara remembered watching him when he ran in the races at school. He flew past all the other kids like a mighty stallion or an eagle in flight. He always had a slick smile plastered on his face as he raced the wind and went far past the finish line. Even with his tall and gangly limbs, you couldn't deny his round shoulders and strong muscles. But he wore his strength so carelessly, like he didn't care much for it or didn't realize he had it.

Twenty minutes. He was so late. She was going to kill him. Amara picked up the bags of fruit and swung them over her shoulders. She stood up to leave.

"I'm here!" a voice called from behind her.

She turned around. Doran was racing up the road. He came into view, and Amara realized with a shock that he had a black eye. The skin around his left eye was swollen and stained with an alarming shade of purple. The bruise was fresh and surrounded the lime green of his eyes like a spreading poison visible through his veins. For some reason, she felt angrier at the sight of it.

"You are late," she said coldly to him.

"I—I know," he said, smiling a little. His smile was a charming thing; just a slight lift of his lips gave a carelessly adorable smile. "I'm sorry. I didn't mean to be late. I was just—"

"You were just what?" She raised her eyebrows at him, not returning his smile.

"I was—" he put one hand through his dirty blond hair. His clothes were messy and torn, his shoes muddy. Amara looked back at his black eye and frowned.

"You want to get into stupid fights with your stupid friends? Don't do it in my shifts. Some of us have places to be and more important things to do. So, I would really appreciate it if you would try and respect other people's time." She thrust the bags of fruit into his arms and walked away.

Chapter Eight

"Hey!" Neo called to Amara as he jumped off the school bench and hurried toward her with a smile on his face.

"Heyyy!" she said, giving him a quick hug and kissing him on the head. "How was your day?" she asked as they walked out of school and headed back to the Children's Home.

"It was great!" he said excitedly, "Well, actually," he considered, "English was *boring* today because we had to read a *boring* text about a *boring* person," he emphasized all the 'borings' in the sentence and attempted to roll his eyes.

Amara stifled a laugh.

"Buuut..." he continued excitedly, "Science was super fun! The Educator taught us about different types of insects, and he actually brought some of them to class and put them in jars!" His chestnut eyes were wide and he moved his tiny hands and jumped around as he talked. "The girls were so scared; it was so funny!" he laughed.

"Oh, I almost forgot," Amara reached into her bag and took out the muffin wrapped in the napkin. She handed it to her brother. "It's from Elianah. They're her mom's famous muffins. Trust me, they are delicious." He took a bite and his freckly face broke into a wide smile. Amara smiled wide herself. She loved his smile. She put her hand on his head and messed up his spikey green hair. As they walked, Neo told her all about the insects they learned about in science through mouthfuls of blueberry.

Another day that week, Amara was also working at the Messenger corral. She had just finished delivering mail and came back to the corral when Messenger Antonio called her.

"Amara, you said that if there were any deliveries to Healer Evetta or Baker Rosemarie's house to assign them to you. Baker Rosemarie ordered some stuff and asked that they be delivered to her house, so I thought I'd ask you if you wanted to take the delivery."

Amara was really surprised he even remembered her asking that. "Yes sure! I'd love to."

"Great," he said. He handed her a cardboard box that had Elianah's address on it. She turned to go but glanced back at Messenger Antonio before heading out, "Thank you," she said.

"No problem," he smiled.

She stood in front of the door to Elianah's house for the second time this week and knocked.

Elianah opened the door, and her face literary lit up with joy when she saw Amara. They walked inside and Elianah placed the cardboard box on the kitchen counter. She took out a jug of orange juice from the fridge and poured some into a glass she handed to Amara and another she held in her hands. They walked into the living room and sat on the big comfy couch. "How is everything?" Elianah asked, and Amara could just catch a hint of hidden concern in her voice, she must still be worried.

"Great," Amara said simply. She took a sip from her glass and tasted the sweet acidic taste of freshly squeezed oranges.

"How was your shift at the Fishing corral the other day?" she asked, "did you run into Lavinia?"

Amara looked down into her glass and turned it slowly in her hands. She watched as its contents swirled around in an endless sea of bright orange.

"What happened?" Elianah asked.

"Nothing happened," Amara lied.

"Mara, I know you, okay? What happened?"

"It was just Lavinia being her old cruel self, that's all. I'm fine."

Elianah opened her mouth to protest but Amara stopped her. "Can we just not talk about it? I want to talk about something else." She put her glass on the table and rested her head back on the pillows. Seconds later, Elianah did the same. "Okay, let's talk about something else."

They both stared at the ceiling in silence for a few moments, and then Elianah spoke. She had a slight smile in her voice. "Remember when we were kids, and you would come over all the time? We used to sneak into the kitchen and steal the cookies my mom made."

Amara gave a small laugh. "One of us would climb over the counter and get the jar out of the cabinet and the other would stand look out."

"Remember what happened when my mom caught us?" Elianah giggled.

"She would make us wash all the dirty dishes."

"And when we finished—"

"She would give each of us a cookie."

They both laughed. They sat there for a while, talking and laughing over bittersweet memories. For a little while, they forgot the troubles and worries of today and sat back and talked about silly things and giggled over stupid jokes together.

Someone knocked loudly on the door. Elianah rushed to open it, Amara right behind her. It was Doran, the boy from the Messenger corral. He was panting, like he ran miles to get here. His face was covered in sweat and his messy honey-colored hair glistened with it. His eyes fell on Amara and he sighed with relief, but that didn't take the worried look off his face. "Thank goodness. I tried looking in the Children's Home and didn't find you there. Then Messenger Antonio told me this was your last delivery so I ran here."

"What is it?" she said anxiously, "did I mess up a delivery or something?"

Doran shook his head. "Educator Kathia sent me. She said your brother collapsed in school."

CHAPTER NINE

Her heart fell into her stomach.

"What?" she said aghast, "When? Why? Where is he now?"

Doran only answered her last question. "He's with Healer Taho. I'm to take you there immediately."

"Then let's go!" she said, angry for some reason. Someone squeezed her shoulder. She looked back and it was Elianah. Amara had almost forgotten she was even there. She looked at her friend fearfully. Elianah smiled encouragingly and nodded as if to tell her that everything's going to be okay. Looking into those gentle and honest eyes, she tried to believe that.

"I'm coming with you," she said and quickly grabbed a coat from behind the door.

They ran as fast as they could with Doran to the hospital. When they reached the place, Amara didn't wait for anyone to open the door or allow her in. She pushed the doors and burst into the room, followed by Elianah. Healer Taho was leaning against a bed. On the bed, there was a boy with spikes of green hair growing out of his head like grass. He was unconscious. Amara slowly approached the bed and put her hand on her little brother's face. It was colder than normal. Her stomach flipped. She turned to the Healer. "What is wrong with him?" she managed to say in a small voice.

"I think you should sit down, my dear," said the old man hoarsely.

"I don't want to sit down. Just tell me what's wrong with him so we can fix it." She tried to sound braver than she felt.

"I am afraid it is something we cannot fix."

"What do you mean 'we cannot fix'? Of course we can!" She was so angry at him for being so ridiculous! If he can't manage to fix whatever it is that needs fixing, she'll just take Neo to Elianah's grandmother. She can cure anything. The old man shook his head, and for a moment, he looked very sad. But Amara didn't care. He was being stupid. What was so wrong with her brother that a simple foul-tasting medicine and two days in bed couldn't fix? Anger was rising in her and she was actually considering waking Neo up and going to Elianah's house right now when the Healer finally spoke.

"He has been touched," he said gravely.

No.

Elianah let out a gasp of horror. Amara's whole body went numb. She couldn't breathe, it was as though all the air had been knocked out of her and she stood there unable to move once more. All the blood drained from her face and it was as white as the bland hospital walls. Her mouth was frozen and her lips slightly parted. Her eyes stared in front of her, wide open with shock. It was as though someone had slapped her senseless.

No. No. No. This couldn't be happening.

He has been touched. The words echoed in her head and she refused to believe them. This was the worst thing that he could've said to her. The Morbus Touch, otherwise known as the Touch of Darkness, could happen to any child under the age of seven. It was a deadly disease that had been spreading in Kumilaka for many years. It caused a marking to appear on a child's skin, but it was a different kind of marking. They called it the marking of death. Which meant the child will not survive past the age of seven. But that couldn't be happening. Not to Neo. He can't have been touched.

"No," Amara said, recovering her voice, "he hasn't been touched."

"I'm afraid he has, my dear child. I am terribly sorry," Healer Taho said.

"No! There must be a mistake. I have done everything to protect him from this! I've made sure he drank a glass of milk every day. I never let him out when the black moon emerges every three months. He hardly ever gets cut and when he does, I clean his wounds right away. He has never eaten black pepper in his life!" She realized she was yelling now but she didn't care. "Fish! He eats fish! I buy it for him every month or so even though it's too expensive. I add more jobs to my schedule so I get paid more and can afford to buy him a coat when winter comes so he doesn't catch a cold!" Now she was crying hysterically. Elianah had walked toward her and put her hands on her shoulders. She was rubbing the small of her back to try and calm her down, but it wasn't working. "I—I—I do everything! Please, Healer, tell me there's been a mistake. This can't be true!"

Healer Taho walked closer to her and spoke in a very gentle tone. "I'm sorry, child. I truly am. But half of the things you mentioned are just myths. They don't stop the Touch. Any child can be touched. We can't predict it and we can't stop or change it. It is not your fault, my dear. There is nothing you could have done to prevent this from happening."

Chapter Ten

Amara was sitting by her little brother's bed. She brushed his grassy hair gently with her hand as he slept. Amara really wished her father could be here right now. He would have somehow made everything better. But he wasn't here. Neither was her mother or Aunt Kaila. It was just her and Neo. Neo was all she had left. He was her only family. She couldn't lose him too. She wouldn't.

"Hey," Elianah walked into the room with a glass of water in her hands. She handed it to Amara and then took a breath before speaking. "I was thinking," she said. She was pulling at one of her blue curls like she always did when she was nervous or distressed. "I think we should go and tell my Nana Eve. She always says that there is hope. There is always a chance we could save the patient. That it wasn't right to give up on people, no matter how hard it is to save them. I know that the Touch is something that can't be cured," she paused for a moment, "but if there is a possibility that Neo could survive, she'll be the one to know."

Amara looked at her for a moment, processing what she was saying, and then stood up quickly. "Yes!" her voice was hoarse and desperate. "Yes, let's go."

"I'll be back," she whispered into her sleeping brother's ear. Then Amara and Elianah both hurried to her house. They went down the hall and knocked on the door that leads into their basement, which they had turned into a clinic after Elianah's grandmother got too old to make everyday trips to the hospital.

"Come in," came her voice from inside.

Amara and Elianah both walked into the room and there, on a small wooden stool, was the person they were here to speak to: Healer Evetta. She was an ancient looking figure. Her hair was gray but still had a few faded purple streaks that were definitely a vibrant shade of violet once, and it was pulled back in a long elegant braid. Her face was lined with wrinkles. But her eyes are what told the story of her age. They were gray, old, wise, and knowing. They were the eyes of someone who had seen many things.

"Hi, Nana Eve," Elianah said tentatively.

"Hello, my dear," Healer Evetta looked up from whatever she was doing and smiled at Elianah warmly. Then she noticed Amara. "Amara, sweetheart! I haven't seen you in a while! Come here my dear, let me see you."

Amara walked toward her. Elianah shut the door behind her and did the same.

"Look at you!" Healer Evetta said happily, turning Amara around. "What a beautiful little lady you have become! How did you manage to grow so fast in a few weeks? It is stunning that gorgeous hair of yours!" She ran her hands through the red flames on Amara's head and then rested them on her cheeks while she looked at her. "Something's wrong," she said in a low voice, looking into the sad blue eyes. Amara opened her mouth to speak but no sound came out. Healer Evetta looked at her granddaughter and saw the same worried expression on her face.

"Oh dear…you sit down, my darlings," she said. She pushed Amara down on the stool and gestured for Elianah to do the same, "and I'm going to make you some of my famous green tea. Trust me; it will make you feel better. Then you can both tell me whatever you came here to say."

A few minutes later, Healer Evetta came back with a tray carrying three mugs of hot tea. She gave one to each of the girls and sat down in front of them with her own mug. Amara took a sip out of her mug and stayed silent. The bittersweet tea flowed through her veins and gave her warmth, strength. Elianah sat quietly beside Amara. It looked as though she wanted to give her the space to talk to Healer Evetta herself, and didn't want to interfere. Healer Evetta didn't talk or rush Amara. She just sat silently with them and drank her own tea.

Amara struggled to form the words in her head. But finally, she took a deep breath and was ready to talk. "My brother Neo," Amara said, "he's been touched." The shock slowly registered onto Healer Evetta's face. Then she covered it with her hands and shook her head in sorrow. "That poor little boy," she said in a brittle voice. Healer Evetta had known both Amara and Neo for a long time. Ever since they were kids, Amara came over to Elianah's house and sometimes brought Neo along to play. She was the closest thing they have ever had to a grandmother. She had treated them both like her own grandchildren and seen them grow up around the house throughout the years.

Amara stared down at her empty mug and started talking fast because if she didn't say it now, she wouldn't be able to. "Healer Taho said there was nothing we can do," she said, "he said that there was no cure for the Morbus Touch and no chance of recovery whatsoever." She could feel a lump rising in her throat. "But… I remember you saying… I remember hearing you say…that there is always hope." Now tears were welling up in her eyes and she tried to blink them away, she was staring at the mug but couldn't see a thing. "I thought—I thought that if there was a chance, any chance at all, that my brother could survive—if—if—" she was scared to say the words, saying them might give her hope. "If maybe there was a cure… I thought you'd be the one who could tell me."

She didn't dare to look up. She didn't want to see the look on Healer Evetta's face, the look of helplessness and pity. The look that said: I'm sorry, dear but there's nothing I can do. The same one Healer Taho had given her. Healer Evetta was quiet for too long. Amara looked up, and to her surprise, she didn't see the look she was expecting. Healer Evetta was looking at Amara as if she was trying to make up her mind. Like there was something she wanted to say but was unsure if she should. Amara didn't say anything. She was going to wait for Healer Evetta to talk when she was ready just like she had waited for her. A few minutes had passed. Healer Evetta had opened her mouth a few times and then closed it as if she had thought better of it. Amara and Elianah both glanced worriedly at each other. Then the old woman buried her face in her hands and shook her head one last time before taking a deep breath just as Amara had done and looking up at the young girl before her.

"There have been rumors," she said softly, "for as long as I could remember, whispers about a cure for the Touch of Darkness. No one speaks loudly of it. It is only spoken about secretly and in the shadows. They say, if we cannot have it, what point is there in spreading the word of it and giving people false hope? It is said to be in the Mountains of Emberose, where grave dangers and wild beasts lie between seeker and treasure. No one dares leave the safe haven of Kumilaka to go in search of the cure. The few brave souls who have ventured outside in the hope of finding it have failed or have never returned." She sighed deeply and placed her hands on Amara's. "Sweet little girl, I am only telling you this because I know what it's like to feel desperate. To hate yourself for not being able to do anything, and have everyone tell you there's absolutely nothing you can do while you watch a loved one die before your eyes. I am not saying the stories are real. After all, I am an old woman who still believes in myths and tales. I am only telling you this to give you a chance to choose. You have the right to know."

Healer Evetta took out a key from her pocket and with it, she opened a drawer from the table sitting beside her. She moved some stuff aside and then took out an old piece of parchment paper and handed it to Amara.

"I've been hearing about this cure for a very long time," she said with a sigh, "and as a Healer, I've seen a countless number of innocent children's lives being slowly taken away because of the Touch. Hearing about the cure, it gave me hope that this disease that has been slithering its way through our land for all those years could be cured somehow. I was determined to find out everything I possibly could about it. I made it my life's mission," she paused for a moment. "But things happen, life doesn't always go to plan. I never got the chance to find out if the cure really exists. I still don't know. And I don't want to feed you lies my sweet little girl, but as I said, you have the right to choose whether to believe them or not."

Then she leaned back on the wall. She looked tired. Amara stood up. She put her mug on the table and looked at the old woman. "Thank you," she said genuinely, "and thank you for the tea." Healer Evetta nodded. The two girls got up, headed back to the door, and opened it, but before stepping out, Amara turned back to the old lady on the stool. They both smiled at each other, sad but knowing smiles.

Chapter Eleven

Elianah was pacing around the kitchen, her face screwed up in thoughtfulness. "But, there's no possible way of getting that cure," she said, running her hands through her baby blue curls in frustration.

"Yes, there is," Amara said in a quiet voice. Her mind was racing. "I can go there. I can get it myself."

Elianah stopped pacing and looked up at Amara. "What? You can't be serious."

"I am. I'm going to go to the Mountains of Emberose and finding the cure. I'll be back before Neo's seventh birthday; I have three and a half months. That's plenty of time."

"But, Mara, that's crazy! You've never left Kumilaka your entire life. You have no idea what's out there. You have absolutely no clue what you're going to find when you reach that place or what dangerous things you'll be facing. You don't even know if the cure actually exists!"

"Eli, don't you see? It's my only chance! Yes, I don't know what's out there and I don't know if I'll find a cure at all. But what other options do I have? Sitting here doing nothing and waiting for Neo to die? I can't live without him, Eli. I can't live with myself knowing that I didn't do every possible thing, tried every last resort, to save him! I have to go. I will go and I will find that cure, for Neo. And if I fail, at least I'd die trying to save my brother instead of letting him die without a fight."

Elianah looked at her for a minute, and then slowly nodded. There were tears in her eyes and she was chewing on her bottom lip like she always did when trying to hold back from crying. "I'm sorry," she said in a wobbly voice, "I'm sorry this happened. You don't deserve this, Mara. You've been through enough already." There was a pause in which Elianah looked at Amara miserably. "I—I can come with you!" she said decidedly. "I know my mother would never allow it but I can sneak out early in the morning or—or pretend that I'm going to the hospital. Then we'll go—we'll go together!" she said it so determinedly but Amara could hear the conviction wavering in her voice.

Amara shook her head firmly. "No. I need you here. I need you to take care of Neo while I'm gone."

Elianah took a shaky breath and then nodded bravely, making her pretty curls bounce more than ever. But after a moment, her eyes started welling up again and she started sniffling and biting her lip in a failed attempt to hold back the uncontrollable sobs that came. She flung her arms around Amara and started crying hard on her shoulder. Amara held tightly to her best friend and felt the tears streaming down her face as well. And as the sun went down, the two best friends stood there, crying into each other's arms and hoping this wasn't a goodbye.

CHAPTER TWELVE

Amara went back to the hospital. The next day, she found Healer Taho in his office and she told him what she had found out. "There is a cure," she said, "there is a cure for the Touch. It is in the Mountains of Emberose and I'm going there to get it."

Healer Taho stared at her in surprise. "You must be joking," he gave out a humorless chuckle, and when she didn't laugh along, he raised his eyebrows at her, "where did you even hear such a thing? This is the stuff of fairytales and stories. It isn't real, and you mustn't believe it is."

"It's Neo's last hope. I'm going and there's nothing you can do to change my mind. I just thought I should let you know." She walked out before he could say anything else. Right as she stepped out of the room, she saw someone standing near the doorway. A skinny girl with navy blue hair stood a few feet away and stared at her. Lavinia. Something hot and sharp moved in the pit of Amara's stomach. She looked at her suspiciously. What was she even doing here? She was probably delivering some fish to the hospital cafeteria. Or was that the Messengers' job? She looked at Lavinia with narrowed eyes, waiting for her to throw another one of her spiteful comments. But she didn't. She just looked at Amara carefully until she walked away.

Amara walked into Neo's room. He was sitting up on his bed and eating from a small bowl of something gooey. "Amara!" he said happily when he saw her, "look what they gave me! Pudding! I've only had pudding once before, remember?"

She sat down on the chair beside his bed, "Yeah, it was on your fifth birthday, right? In Elianah's house. I remember

Eli was so excited to give it to you that she almost dropped the tray when she came in!" Amara laughed.

"Yes!" Neo giggled, "and—and you ate half of yours and wanted to save the rest so you hid it from me but I found it and ate the whole thing!"

"Ha! I forgot about that! You owe me half of that pudding, you little thief!" She reached for his bowl. Neo held it out of her reach.

"Half a spoon," he said, raising his tiny arms as far as they would go to protect his pudding.

"Three!" Amara bargained.

"One."

"Two and we'll call it a deal." She held out her hand.

He shook it and gave her the spoon. She put a spoonful of the creamy chocolate in her mouth and it brought back sweet memories. "You know what?" she said swallowing, "I don't think that was the only time you've had pudding. Dad and Aunt Kaila used to bring some to us when we were little. I think you might've had it a couple of times before. But you don't remember it."

"Maybe," he shrugged, "Just like I don't remember Dad."

Amara looked at him sadly. She squeezed herself into the bed and sat there with him. They both lay back on the soft pillows. From under her shirt, she pulled out a necklace that was hanging around her neck. She turned the locket between her fingers and examined it. A round golden pendant with a rose engraved on it hung at the end of a long chain. It was an old rusty thing. She doubted it had any real value at all. Inside it was a picture of their family, their family before.

"This is him," Amara said softly to Neo, pointing at her father's picture inside the locket. Of course, Neo had seen it many times before, but he was always somehow comforted when Amara talked about their father or told him random things about him. "He had a sweet tooth," she laughed, "and would always love making excuses to get any kind of dessert into the house. Mom used to get mad at him."

Her mother had given her this locket after her seventh birthday. When she'd given it to her, she had said: "As long as you have this, you'll know I'll always be with you, my little flame of fire." She used to call Amara that, she said it's because she lighted up her life. Her life, the one that was over before she could see her little baby boy take his first steps and raise him until he grew up to be the amazing brave boy he was and the great man he'll become. The man he *will* become, because Amara will find that cure. She will save him.

"What were you talking to Healer Taho about?" Neo asked suddenly, as though he had read her mind.

"How did you—?"

"I asked one of the Healers if she has seen you around and she said you were talking to Healer Taho about something and you'll be here in a bit."

"Neo—"

"What's wrong with me, Amara?" he looked at her with those big teary eyes, the innocent eyes of a little boy, just a little boy. "Am I sick? Can they make me better?"

A small sob escaped her lips. It was time. She had to tell him. Amara held her brother's tiny hands in hers. "Neo," she said slowly, "Healer Taho told me, the day you were brought here, that you have been touched by the Touch of Morbus." She saw a flicker of fear in the chestnut eyes, he must have heard stories about it at school. She went on, "They say there's no medicine to make you better. But I heard about a cure, a cure that can be found far away from here. And I'm going to find it."

Neo looked at her. He was slowly processing what he'd just heard. After a moment, he started shaking his head. "No," he said fearfully, "no, you can't go. You can't leave me."

"I have to, Neo! It's the only way to find a cure for you."

"No!" he said loudly, "you can't leave. Please don't go. I need you, Amara. Please," he was crying like a baby and shaking his head forcefully as if he could make all this go away. "Please. Please don't. Please," he begged. Just like Amara had begged her father once.

She held him firmly by the shoulders and looked him in the eye. "Neo," she said as she did her best to hold back her tears, "listen to me. I don't want to leave. But this is the only way I can save you. Can you trust me? Can you trust that I'll do everything in my power to go get the cure and come back to you?"

With wet eyes and tears streaming down his beautiful freckly face, he nodded.

Chapter Thirteen

In the cafeteria, Amara was trying to get some food for her last dinner with her brother before going in search for the cure. But all she could think about was how she was going to get to the Mountains of Emberose. She was supposedly leaving tomorrow morning, in the hope of making it back as soon as possible. But she had no idea what to do.

Amara was holding out the ladle to put some of the nasty mashed potatoes onto her plate when she noticed someone standing by the door watching her. It was Lavinia, again. She turned around to face her; from experience she had learned, it was never wise to give your back to Lavinia. She looked around and the dining hall was completely empty except for the two of them. She watched her from across the room. Nothing, Lavinia said nothing. Lavinia never says nothing! Not to Amara at least. When they saw each other at school, she always had to say something mean or 'accidently' trip Amara, and if they pass each other in the market, she'd have to make a snide remark or give a hateful comment. Often times, she did much worse. Yet now, she said nothing for their second meeting today. She just looked carefully at Amara as she had done earlier. There was something very wrong about that. Amara placed her tray on one of the tables and walked toward Lavinia. "Is something wrong?" she said in a mockingly pleasant voice, not able to disguise the tone of anger in it. "You've been staring at me all day."

Lavinia opened her mouth to say something but closed it again as if she'd lost the nerve. This was too weird. As Amara stared at her, she noticed that Lavinia was acting nervous. Her hands were clenched into tight fists and her shoulders were tensed up. She had something to say but she really didn't want to say it. And Amara couldn't help but find this oddly satisfying. She raised her eyebrows at Lavinia as if to tell her to spit it out.

"I—I heard you talking to Healer Taho," she said tentatively, so unlike Lavinia. Amara had never seen her act that way. She was always so sure of herself. But right now, she just looked scared. "About a—a cure for the Touch and how you want to go and find it in the Mountains of Emberose. And I want to come with you."

What?

"Why on earth would you want to do that?" Amara asked, bewildered.

"Because…" she took a shaky breath, "Zuri, my little sister, she's been touched. She's only just five and it's not fair. I want to come and help you find the cure so I can save her."

Amara gaped at her. She hadn't seen that coming.

"My mom has given up on any hope for saving her, and her dad—"

"Her dad?" Amara questioned.

Lavinia ignored her. "So? Are we going?"

Are we going? She must be joking. Amara couldn't help but laugh.

"And why would I even consider taking your help after you've been so awful to me all this time?" Amara said.

"Because," she said determinately, "we both want the same thing, to save our little brother and sister from that *evil* thing." She said that with disgust in her voice and Amara had to agree, "We might have had our differences, but this is bigger than that! You can't do this on your own and you know it. I'm not saying we should be best buddies and hold each other's hands and sing happy songs on the way, believe me, I'm the last to want that. I'm just saying that I need your help in this and you need mine. Besides, have you even figured out how you're going to get there? I have my father's boat and I can sail it."

This was true. She didn't have any other way to get there. Maybe she did need Lavinia's help, as awful as it would be to have her company. But she had to think of the best way to get that cure and save Neo, and so far, this was it. Before she could talk herself out of it, she said: "Fine."

"Good," said Lavinia.

"Can you get the boat ready by tomorrow morning?"

"Yeah, sure, I can do that."

"We leave first thing tomorrow. Get everything you need for the journey ready; food, water, and clothes, whatever."

Lavinia nodded. Then she turned around and left.

Amara couldn't believe what she had just done. She agreed to go on this crazy journey with the person she probably hated most in the world. What was she thinking?

When Amara went back to the room, she found Neo fast asleep. He looked like a little angel. His tiny body was cocooned on the corner of the large bed. His lips were slightly parted and he was breathing slowly and heavily. She noticed that his face was still covered in smears of chocolate from the pudding he had eaten earlier. She walked closer to him and gently wiped the chocolate off his face. Then, she quietly climbed up the big hospital bed and took him in her arms. Amara cradled her little brother as he slept, and made him promises she hoped she could keep.

Chapter Fourteen

Amara opened her eyes and her heart tightened in her chest as realization washed over her. It was morning. It was time. She turned her head and saw Neo sleeping in her arms. She stayed like that for a moment and wished that she could go back to sleep and never leave his side. But she had to. She got up from the bed and picked up everything she might need from here. The rest she was taking from her room at the Children's Home and then she will go back to her old house to pack up some other things she might need. Then she looked at Neo. She was going to have to wake him up to say goodbye. But first, she just stood there watching him. She had to be brave for him.

She gently shook him awake. "Neo, Neo, wake up." At first, he slowly opened his eyes and looked at her tiredly, then his eyes widened in realization. He jumped up from bed.

"Amara!"

"It's okay, it's okay. I'm still here."

He let out a breath of relief.

"But I have to leave now."

"No!"

"Neo, we've talked about this. I have to leave as soon as possible to come back before the three months are over. I have to leave now." As she said that, she felt her heart being squeezed tighter in her chest. She walked toward Neo and lowered herself down to him. "I'm coming back, Neo," she whispered.

"You promise?"

She knew, better than anyone, that she shouldn't make him promises she couldn't keep. She shouldn't. "I do," she said in a strangled voice.

He nodded, tears falling from his eyes again.

She held his little face in her hands, wiping the tears staining his chubby cheeks with her thumbs. Amara stayed there for a whole minute, just looked at the blotchy red face of her little brother, and took it in for the last time. She looked at the trembling pink lips, felt the roundness of those beautiful cheeks, counted the freckles on his nose, and wiped the messy spikes of grass-green hair covering his big sad chestnut eyes.

Then she held him tightly in her arms and Neo hugged her back, putting his little thin arms around her neck.

"I will miss you," he sobbed.

"Me too. Me too, my little baby. It'll be alright," she said comfortingly.

Amara rubbed his back soothingly like she had always done when he got hurt or came home crying. He then slowly pulled himself out of her embrace.

"Before you go…" He wiped his face with his sleeves and took something out of his pocket to give to her. It was a folded piece of paper. She opened it. There was a pretty crayon-colored drawing of a little boy with spikey green hair and a girl with flames of red. They stood holding hands and smiling. It was something about this simple piece of art that just made her eyes flood with tears.

"But you can't have it now," Neo said, "I still haven't colored the trees in the back so it's not done yet. I'll give it to you when you come back."

Her amazing little boy. When did he become so grown up? Amara will find that cure. She will come back to him.

Amara looked up at Neo and nodded. "Thank you," she said and her voice cracked just a little.

He nodded back bravely. Then she kissed the top of his head – letting her lips linger a moment too long on the spikey hair – and walked out the room.

Chapter Fifteen

Amara went back to the Children's Home to pack everything she might need from there. Some changes of clothes, food she bought with the little money that she'd saved, a big bottle she filled with water, and a pocketknife her father had given her when she turned eight. She found the piece of parchment Healer Evetta had given her inside her pocket. It was a map, a map to the Mountains of Emberose. She put it in the bag as well.

"Amara," Sev, the brown boy with the silver afro, had just walked into their room.

"Hey," she said awkwardly as she pulled the packed bag over her shoulders. She wasn't exactly planning on telling anyone she was leaving.

"I heard about Neo," he said, and he looked genuinely miserable. "That really sucks," he rolled his eyes and gave a shaky laugh, empty of humor. Amara had a feeling he was trying to fight the urge to cry. She was a little shocked that Sev really cared that much about Neo. But now that she thought about it, they had been roommates and known each other for over three years. It made sense that he did. "I just wanted to say that I'm sorry. And—um—Jovie and I were planning to head down to the hospital today after training to see Neo, if that's okay with you, of course."

Amara nodded. "It is, of course it is. You can go see him whenever you want. He'd really like that."

"Great," Sev nodded gladly. She felt a lot better, knowing that Neo will have company while she's gone.

Jovie walked into the room. "You're leaving?" she asked as soon as she saw the bag on Amara's shoulders.

"Um—yeah," Amara wasn't exactly sure if she was asking about leaving the Children's Home or Kumilaka. But she didn't feel like explaining right now.

Jovie looked at her sadly. "I'm gonna miss you."

"You are?"

Jovie looked surprised that Amara would ask that question.

"You bet I would," she said with a little smile on her face, "who's gonna rant about Coreen with me? Or cover up for me when I sneak out? Or stay up 'til after midnight and talk about silly stuff until Tarra throws pillows at us?"

Amara laughed at that. "I'll be back," she said.

"Can't wait," Jovie gave Amara a hug, "and don't worry about Neo, it'll all be all right in the end," she said in a low voice as she held Amara into the hug.

"I have to go now," she said, pulling back, "see you guys later." She had to go and find a way to escape the place without anyone noticing that she was leaving. She was already running late and didn't have time for any questioning, and there will be a lot of that if they found out where she was really planning to go.

Amara was about to walk out the door when Jovie spoke, "Carer Romar is pacing the halls downstairs. I think he'll be a little suspicious if he saw you walking out of the building with all your stuff packed in a bag."

"Yeah," Sev said, "but don't you think it'll be okay if she told them she was going to stay with Neo in the hospital?"

"Maybe," Jovie shrugged, then she looked at Amara, "but it doesn't really look like she's planning to stay at the hospital, does it?"

Sev looked From Jovie to Amara to the big bag on her shoulders. Amara waited for them to ask her where she was really going. Instead, Jovie said, "We can help you sneak out."

"I can distract Carer Romar," Sev suggested.

"And we also have to make sure Coreen doesn't see you because she's bound to go report you straight away," Jovie added.

"Are you guys sure?" Amara asked uncertainly.

"Yes," Jovie said, "but we have to hurry, come on."

As soon as they walked out of the room, they heard Coreen's voice from down the hall. She was shouting at some of the kids for running down the stairs.

"Quick, hide," Jovie said right away.

Sev pushed her into a corner and then walked toward Coreen. He said something to her that made her grab his arm and storm down the hall and into one of the boys' rooms. He'd probably told her a lie about something to drive her away. Jovie took Amara's hand and pulled her down the stairs. They hurried down the long flight of stairs and reached the entrance hall of the building, where kids were running around after breakfast and getting ready to head out for school and training, and a couple of Carers stood on watch. Amara stood concealed behind Jovie to hide the fact that she was carrying all her belongings on her back, which pretty much gave away her plan to escape.

"Get ready to run," Jovie whispered. Without another word, she went to stand in the middle of the room and yelled before pretending to faint and falling to the floor. Both the Carers hurried to see what was wrong, and that's when Amara ran. She ran past the distracted Carers and to the giant wooden doors of the Children's Home. Before walking out of the gates, she took one last glance at the girl being helped up by two Carers. Jovie winked at her. As Amara finally walked out of the Children's Home, she found herself really hoping to see them all again.

When she reached her old house, she noticed that the sun was high up in the sky and it was a bright and lovely day. She looked at the old house from afar. The ancient wood was chipped and battered at certain spots but still held up the house firmly. The old peeled off paint was the color of faded red. There were two windows – too dirty to look through – and one of them had a long crack running down the middle where half the glass had shattered. The door was a big brown one. The low roof was filled with leaves, falling from the trees covering the house and concealing it between their branches. Amara walked to the broken window and jumped through it.

She was inside her childhood home again. But there wasn't enough time for sentiment. She picked up some extra essentials, took her father's bow and arrows from where she hid them, and shoved them all into her overly full bag. After quickly getting dressed for the trip, she brushed her flaming red hair back into a ponytail, hid her mother's locket under her shirt, put on the oversized coat that used to belong to her father, carried the bag, and left her home, wishing with all her heart that she would return to it once more.

Chapter Sixteen

Now Amara had to go and meet up with Lavinia by her father's boat. That would be by the sea, the Fisher corral area. She walked and walked and kept turning around, feeling that someone was following her. She was imagining it, maybe she was wishing that someone would follow and stop her from going. But she had to do this. She had to be brave, for Neo.

She reached the shore and saw that on one edge there was a big, old, and beautiful fishing boat floating in the water and ready for sail. She walked closer to it. "Lavinia?" she said loudly.

"I'm here!" Lavinia jumped out of the boat. "It took you long enough!"

Amara ignored that. "Are we ready to go?" she asked coldly.

"Yeah, pretty much," answered Lavinia, equally cold.

"Then let's get on the boat."

"Wait!" said someone from behind them.

They both turned around. There was no one. Then someone came out from behind a tree. A tall figure with long and gangly limbs, messy honey-colored hair, and brilliant green eyes stood before them. He had a long nose, thin mouth, a broad good-natured smile that revealed a single crooked tooth sitting between its straight and white neighbors. Between his thick dark eyebrows was a marking partly covered by his wild straws of hair but could still be clearly seen as the marking of a Messenger: Doran.

"What are you doing here?" Amara said, surprised. "Wait, were you the one following me all this time?" she added angrily.

"Um, so you noticed?" He scratched the back of his head and smiled nervously. She noticed that the swelling around his injured eye had decreased and it had turned from the dark shade of purple it was to a light yellowish-green. "I'm sorry! I didn't mean to scare you or anything. I just—"

"You just what?" she asked. Her tone was cold; she still hadn't quite forgiven him for keeping her waiting that other time.

"I wanted to ask you something."

"Ask me something? This isn't the greatest time to talk really. We have to go." She turned back to the boat.

"Wait!" he yelled again, "I want to come with you!"

Not again!

"What?" Amara and Lavinia said together.

"I want to come with you both, to go with you to the Mountains of Emberose."

"How on earth do you know where we're going?" said Lavinia, stepping closer and crossing her arms.

"I might have accidentally heard you two talking about it in the cafeteria when I was delivering some supplies in the back," he mumbled.

"You what?!" Amara shouted, "what is it with you people and eavesdropping?" She waved her arms at Lavinia and Doran exasperatedly.

"I'm sorry!" he said again, "I know I shouldn't have but I just couldn't help hearing and… I wanna go with you."

"Why do you even want to go, delivery boy?" Lavinia shot at him.

"I—I want to leave Kumilaka. Just once." He had a small smile on his lips and he was looking at something in the far distance that Amara couldn't see. "I want to go on an adventure," he said fiercely, sounding for a moment like a little boy with wild dreams. "And what a better one to go on than the one that could possibly save two innocent children from a merciless disease?" He looked back at Amara. "Please, let me come along. You girls need the company of a man. I could help you with some of the rough things and give you a hand when it gets hard."

"Yeah, right!" Lavinia snorted, clearly finding this ridiculously amusing. "A man, he says! Well, thank you for offering your gracious services but I believe us two 'helpless' girls will do just fine without your masculine assistance. Let's go, we already took too long." She turned back and walked to the boat.

Amara was still looking at Doran, whose smile faltered slightly.

"Okay," she said.

"Really?" Doran said excitedly.

"What?" came Lavinia's shocked voice from behind.

"But before you decide to come on this with us, there are a few things you need to know," she said warningly, feeling like she was going to regret this. "Once this boat sails, there's no turning back. You can't change your mind and you can't go back no matter what. Unless you want to swim back to Kumilaka, in that case, I don't mind. If you're coming, you're going to help us in whatever way we need you to. This is not a happy adventure from a children's book you read. This is a serious journey. We have a goal and we don't know what kind of crazy and dangerous things we're going to face trying to reach it. We might not even make it back," she forced out, then added, "is your family okay with you going on an *adventure*?" She rolled her eyes.

Doran nodded, not bothering to hide his excitement. "I know. I'm ready to face whatever comes in our way and I'm very much willing to help you in anything you want. I live with my uncle, and I'm pretty sure he wouldn't even notice I'm gone or care if I don't come back. In fact, he might be quite happy I took off, one less mouth to feed, right?" he smiled carelessly, but Amara heard the bitterness in his voice.

"Okay," Amara said, "good. Lavinia, how many cabins are there on the boat?"

"You aren't serious, are you?" Lavinia said, gaping at her.

"Yes, I am. So, how many?"

"Two."

"You take one and Lavinia and I can share the other," she said to Doran.

"Who said anything about sharing a room?" Lavinia said angrily.

"I did, just now. Can we go now?"

"No, we can't go!" Lavinia shouted, "it is bad enough that I have to go with you, but share a cabin and have mailboy over there come too? No way!"

"You don't *have* to go with me. You're the one who asked to come along!" Amara shouted back.

"Don't act like you're babysitting me! I have the boat, remember? Without me, you'll still be at the hospital trying to figure out how to get there!"

"Ha! As if you could do any better! A boat isn't that hard to find you know. But you know what is? A map! And if I'm not mistaken, I'm the one who has it! So, if you changed your mind and don't want to come along, then fine! Go take your precious boat and get lost in the sea, see if I care. I'll find another one and go to the mountains without you!"

That sure shut her up. Lavinia's face was twisted with anger and she looked like she wanted to bite Amara's head off. But she stood there with her arms crossed, silent.

"Now can we go?"

Lavinia gave Doran one last look of hatred and then got up on the boat.

Amara followed but before she got on the boat Doran stopped her.

"Amara," he said, giving her a sincere smile, "thank you."

Chapter Seventeen

They were sailing away from Kumilaka. It was the first time Amara had seen the whole land like this. Birds were soaring high over the land of beauty, the land of color: the beautiful green of a thousand trees, the bright yellow of cornfields, the faded red and blue of the houses, and the glittering gold of the sand. Pretty little horses were crossing the roads and pulling carriages, cows were roaming through fields of green. Amara stood and watched as her home became smaller and smaller as the boat moved further and further away. She stood there and watched until Kumilaka became a mere speck in the distance, lost in the brilliant blue of the sea.

"It's strange, isn't it? Leaving home?" Doran was standing right behind her all this time and she hadn't noticed.

"Yeah," she said, and her voice was surprisingly hoarse. She cleared her throat, "Yeah, it is."

"I've always wanted to leave, it's always been my dream to sail away from that place and go on a journey to somewhere, anywhere. I used to daydream about it all the time and my uncle would get mad at me. I used to wish for this very moment every single night. Here it is, but it's still strange, leaving."

Amara and Doran opened the trapdoor on the floor of the boat and got down the ladder. There were two cabins indeed, both extremely small though. Doran took the smaller one and Amara went into the slightly bigger one to share with Lavinia. The room was ancient, the wooden floorboards were scratched, and the faded yellow paint was pealed. The air had a mixture of odd smells: dust, old bed sheets, cigarettes, sea salt, and a nasty smell that Amara suspected was mold. It was also tiny, with barely enough room to hold the two rusty old beds that were taking up all its space. The only other thing in the room was a large trunk sitting in front of one of the beds. Amara took the other one. She placed her bag on the foot of her bed and went back up the ladder.

They sailed for hours and hours until it got dark. All day, Lavinia gave both Amara and Doran lessons on how to sail the boat. Just so they can all take shifts keeping an eye on the wheel. They pretty much got the hang of it but Lavinia said she was going to give them one last round of lessons tomorrow just to make sure, and she took this night's shift.

Amara went back to her room and sat on the bed. Its rusty springs gave a loud squeak. She pulled off her father's coat and her jacket and threw them over her bag on the floor. Kicking off her boots, she lied down on the bed without bothering to change into any other clothes.

Amara stayed like that for hours: lying in bed wide awake, her head swarming with questions, doubts, and fears. She somehow couldn't believe that she was sailing over the ocean now, miles and miles away from home. This was the biggest thing she had ever done in her life. And though her heart was yelling with fear and her uneasy stomach was threatening to make her puke at any moment, she couldn't help but notice the tiny sense of excitement dancing somewhere inside of her. At some point, she drifted off to sleep, but her dreams weren't any less frightening.

Chapter Eighteen

The door of the room creaked open and then slammed shut. Someone threw themselves on the other bed in the room. Moments later, there was the sound of heavy breathing and low snoring. Amara opened her eyes and found Lavinia sleeping on her stomach at the bed next to hers. She must have been awake all that time steering the boat. Amara got up and headed into the bathroom outside the bedroom cabins. It was a small thing with barely enough room to stand. She changed into her second set of clothes and washed her face. Then she looked into the little round mirror above the sink. Ocean blue eyes stared back at her. Her fiery red hair – messy from sleep – was as radiant as always. Orange and yellow streaks glowed in between the red ones. Amara slid her fingers through her hair to try and smooth it out and free it from tangles – she hadn't thought to bring a hairbrush with her – and then fixed it into a braid and hastily covered the marking on her forehead with her uneven bangs. The slightly shorter side didn't manage to cover the scar on her left brow. The one she got two years ago…

Amara was on her way back to the Children's Home. She had had a bad day at training that day. She wasn't good at any of the corrals no matter how hard she tried. For once, she'd like to be good at something. Amara ran back to her old house and jumped through the broken window. Every time she came back here, she thought the house looked smaller than she remembered it. But it was still her home, just as she left it, except for the dust that had swallowed the furniture and the cobwebs that filled the corners of the walls. She went to the ancient closet that was in her parents' old room and opened it to find a ragged brown bag. Inside that bag was what she was looking for, her father's bow and arrows.

When Amara was little, her father had taught her how to use a bow and arrow, and she was quite good at it. Well, at least when she practiced shooting at a tree. Of course, when her father had tried to train her with him in the Hunter corral after the town meeting it didn't go that well, but she was only seven back then. Now she was eleven years old – and turning twelve soon – so she could surely handle it now. Amara was yearning to prove herself. She wanted to do something – anything – right. She had to be good at something; she just didn't know what it was yet. So, she took her father's hunting bag and ran into the arms of the forest. She walked slowly between the trees, listening to the sound of a hundred birds tweeting and chirping. The sun was emerging behind the trees, casting beams of light all around. Amara loved being in here. It reminded her of the days of her childhood, the long afternoons she spent here with her father, the songs they sang, the games they played. It reminded her, what it was like to be happy and safe…but those days are gone now. She pulled the weapon out from the bag and did as her father had once trained her to do.

She was standing, hidden. An animal was thirty yards away, clueless. She slowly raised her bow, arrow poised. She steadied her breath and concentrated on nothing but the arrow and her target. It was in a perfect position to shoot, to kill. This was her chance, her chance to do something right for a change. This was her chance to prove everyone wrong, to prove herself to them. She just had to let go. Just let go, and end its life. Her face was drenched in sweat. Her heart was beating in full speed against her chest. Her arms and legs shook madly. Just shoot. Just kill. Her father's voice rang in her head. It won't feel a thing. She moved the bow to the far left and shot the arrow into the air at nothing. Losing control of the bow and yelling in frustration, fear, and anger, she fell onto the ground and hit the side of her head on a sharp rock. It cut through her skin and then blood was running down her face. She shoved the bow and arrows into the bag and ran out of the forest and into the warmth of Elianah's house, where Healer Evetta stitched up her wound.

That was how she got it, the scar on her left brow. It was a constant reminder of many things. Her weakness, how different she was from her father and her failure in doing anything right. She even failed in protecting Neo. How was she ever going to save him if all she could do all those years was fail? She couldn't even shoot a stupid arrow like her father did.

No. She can't think that way. Why would she even want to be like her father, the father who abandoned them, the father who left them all alone? She used to look up to him, think he was the best father in the entire universe, but now, all she could feel toward him was anger. He left them all alone. But was she any better? She left Neo. She left her little brother, her only family, all alone when he needed her the most. NO. She did not leave him. She did not fail in protecting him. She is going to find that cure and go back to save him. Nothing will stop her. She had promised.

Amara walked out of the bathroom, climbed up the ladder, and opened the trapdoor to be greeted by a breeze of salty air. Doran was standing by the steering wheel. He turned around when he heard her coming up.

"Good morning!" he said, shooting her a radiant smile. How this boy doesn't run out of smiles she'll never know. He had a million different smiles and he gave them out like candy.

"Morning," she said back.

"Finally, I have someone to talk to! Lavinia ran down to her cabin as soon as she saw me to go to sleep, and I can't say I blame her. She was out here all night, and it gets quite lonely. Also, the sound of the waves sure puts you to sleep, especially if you were wide awake all night."

"You didn't sleep last night?" Amara asked. She was awake a long time and hadn't heard a sound coming from his cabin so she'd assumed he was sound asleep the whole time.

"Umm—no. It was our first night out of Kumilaka and I—err—didn't want to—err—I wanted to enjoy it," he said finally, and from his tone, Amara understood he didn't want to talk further about it.

After a slightly long pause, he talked again, "Don't get me wrong, I don't mean I don't like it here. I love it, actually. Look at this sight, isn't it gorgeous!" He waved his long arms around him.

Amara looked around, and for the first time, she started to appreciate the beauty of the ocean they were sailing through. She looked at the endless sea of blue. Its turquoise waves were gently crashing against each other. Shifting around calmly and dancing gracefully. The golden glow of the sun shined through the rippling water. The whooshing sound of the waves being carried by the wind on the surface of the ocean and the soft buzzing that came from its depths calmed Amara. For a moment, as she slowly breathed in the fresh and salty air around her, her head was clear from all worries and fears. She was a mere soul lost in the beauty of the peaceful yet powerful ocean.

"Yeah," she whispered, not wanting to spoil the beauty of the moment, "it sure is."

Chapter Nineteen

It was late afternoon and Amara was starving. She was trying not to think about food because she barely had enough. Doran – who was still standing by the steering wheel – stretched and gave out a loud sigh.

"Can you maybe take a hold of the wheel for a second?" he said to Amara, "I want to get some lunch."

"Sure," Amara took his place as he picked his bag from the floor, swung it over his shoulder, and went down to his cabin. He came back seconds later and had something wrapped with brown paper in his hands.

"Thanks," he said and stood back by the wheel.

Even though Amara wanted to save her food, Doran had mentioned lunch and she was even hungrier now. So, she thought it was a good time to eat something. She sat, cross-legged, on the wooden floor of the deck and took out a banana she had packed in her bag and started peeling it off. It had some brown patches on it but was still considered fresh because she had only gotten it yesterday when she'd passed the market early in the morning. She managed to take small bites to fool herself into thinking it was more food than it actually was. Doran – who had one hand on the steering wheel and his back to Amara – glanced at her.

"What *are* you doing?" he said with his mouth full, trying to hide his smile but failing.

"What does it look like I'm doing?" Amara said annoyed, "I'm having lunch."

He swallowed. "This is not lunch. A banana, seriously?"

"Why do you care what I eat?" She scowled at him.

Doran laughed and turned away from her. A few seconds later, he threw something at her.

"Hey!" she shouted, catching it in the last second. "What was that for?" she said. She stared at the brown wrapping in her hands.

"My friend Merlo makes the best sandwiches in the world," he said and turned his head to look at her. "I went by to his place yesterday to tell him I might be going away, you know, if you agree to let me come along and—"

"What does that—?" she started.

"Eat," he said simply, facing the front again.

She looked down at her hands for a moment then took off the brown wrapping. It was half a sandwich. A turkey and cheese sandwich, with beautiful sliced turkey, thin slices of cheese, lettuce and tomato, a light layer of mayo, and a couple of bacon strips, all layered – delicious looking – inside two toasts of bread. Amara's mouth was watering just by looking at this gorgeous thing. But she was being silly.

"Doran…" she said, looking at him.

He pretended not to hear her. She looked at the sandwich in her hands, but hesitated. She looked at Doran again, but he was stubborn.

She sighed and then took a bite out of the sandwich. The toast was a little hard, but the mixture of flavor that danced around in Amara's mouth made her close her eyes and smile. It was an explosion of flavor: the taste of the delicate turkey, the sweet tomatoes, the salty cheese, and the creamy texture of the mayonnaise. Amara tilted her head back and let it all sink in; she hadn't had any decent food in a while, unless you count the hospital cafeteria food, which she certainly didn't.

"Thanks," she said gratefully, her head still leaned back. She still couldn't see Doran's face but somehow, she knew he was smiling.

The trapdoor opened and Lavinia came out.

"Good morning!" Doran greeted her with a friendly smile.

Lavinia rolled her eyes at him and grunted. She pushed him out of her way and stood in front of the steering wheel. "Stop saying that every time you see me."

"What, good morning?" Doran asked, puzzled.

"What do you think, smiley face?"

"But why?" Doran smiled at her again.

"Because it's annoying, and it's not even morning! Plus, your stupid smiles might be contagious," she muttered the last thing and rolled her eyes. "Now shut up!" She turned to Amara, "Give me the map."

Amara hesitated.

Lavinia raised her eyebrows at her. "What? Are you afraid I'd steal the map, throw you both off the boat, and take off?"

Amara wouldn't really put it past her. "Well—maybe."

Lavinia shot her a vicious smile. "Well, good," she said mockingly, "'cause I just might."

Amara grudgingly handed her the map. Lavinia pulled it out of her hands. Doran looked at Amara and shrugged his shoulders with an amused smile.

After a few minutes, Lavinia pulled her head up from whatever it is she was doing. "Okay, that looks about right," she murmured to herself, taking one last look at the map. Then she looked back at the other two, "I'll take it from here. Redhead, you can take tonight's shift."

When it was Amara's turn to take over the wheel, Lavinia and Doran headed down to their cabins.

"Don't you dare snooze off!" Lavinia called as she disappeared down the trapdoor.

"Good luck!" Doran said and followed her down.

Amara stood there and put her hands on the wheel. It was so quiet, nothing but the sound of the blowing wind carrying the ocean waves: so calming, so relaxing. The sky was filled with thousands, millions of stars. It looked as though droplets of white paint were splattered all over a huge midnight blue canvas. The moon hung in the sky like a glowing silver orb. Its light glistened on the surface of the royal blue water.

It was hard to believe that the same starry sky and the same silvery moon were sitting over Kumilaka. It seemed as if Amara had sailed into a different universe.

A shudder went through Amara's body. She looked around to try and see what could've caused it. She couldn't see a thing. She actually couldn't see a thing. Everything had turned black. It was as if someone had turned off the light of the moon. She looked up. Clouds were covering it and concealing its shining light. Amara felt another cold shiver run down her body. Darkness, darkness was all she could see. Pitch black darkness. It made her uneasy. She stood there trying to think of anything else while she waited for the stupid clouds to move.

They finally did, but the feeling of uneasiness still filled Amara from her head to her toes. She felt cold and lonely. Taking the locket out from under her shirt, she opened it carefully. At one side was a picture of her mother and father on their wedding day. They looked so young and happy. Her mother had short red hair that was as striking as Amara's, she looked up at her husband with big chestnut eyes filled with love. Her father looked tall and strong, he held his wife lovingly between his arms. His hair had been recently shaved and had a darker shade of green than Neo's. At the other side was a picture of Amara. She was a little thing, only four or five. Her hair was shoulder-length and she didn't have bangs that covered her forehead. She had a wide smile and her big eyes were filled with happiness. If she lifted the picture of herself, she'd find a picture of Neo, still a newborn. He had little sprouts of green growing from his head. His chestnut eyes were open wide with innocent curiosity.

She looked back at her mother's face. One of the things she remembered loving most about her mother was her voice. She had the most beautiful voice. Amara remembered when she used to sing her to sleep. Her voice was angelic. Listening to her mother sing always made her feel like there was nothing else in the entire world but her, her mother, and that gorgeous voice of hers. It was like those moments lasted forever. Amara would lie there, listening to her mother, feeling her gentle hands brushing back her hair, and she could feel it, the love. It was vibrating through every inch of air in the room and surrounding them, engulfing them with its intensity. She could feel it in her mother's touch against her skin, in her good night kiss on her forehead. She could feel it in her voice as it echoed through the room and soared high above all time and space. Amara would let her heavy eyelids fall. The last thing she'd see was her mother, her beautiful face looking at her with big chestnut eyes filled with infinite and unconditional love. And as she drifted to sleep, she'd hear her mother's voice sing her to the land of dreams. It soothed her and wrapped her body safe while her mind slipped into another universe. Even as she dreamt, a little part of her would hear her mother's voice whisper her good night.

"I'll always be with you," her mother had said. She didn't feel like anyone was with her right now though. She felt miserable and utterly alone, in the middle of the sea on a dark and chilly night.

Chapter Twenty

It was morning. Amara had just started to feel sleepy when Lavinia came up. "Delivery boy down there is such a noisy sleeper!" she said, annoyed, as soon as she saw Amara.

"What?" Amara muttered, struggling to keep her eyes open.

"Ha!" Lavinia smiled nastily, "good luck with sleeping. But lucky you, he's gonna be up here in a bit."

Amara had no idea what Lavinia was talking about but she was too tired to bother. She headed down to her cabin, closed the door, and fell on the bed. Her eyes fell closed and she was just drifting to sleep when she heard loud noises coming from the other side of the wall, like someone was shifting madly on the bed in the other room, whose springs were screeching noisily. After a short while it stopped, and Amara heard quiet footsteps, the door of the next door's cabin open and slam shut, and then what she thought must be the bathroom door do the same. She then fell asleep.

Amara woke with a start. She thought she felt her bed move, but she was only imagining. She walked up to the deck. The sky looked darker than usual and she could see gray clouds slowly approaching them from afar.

"What's going on?" she said, starting to feel anxious.

"Lavinia says a storm might be coming," Doran answered her, looking up at the sky.

"I never said it *might* be coming!" Lavinia said loudly. "It is! Can't you see the sky? A dim-witted Laborer could've told you that, mail boy! Or were you two expecting a nice and peaceful trip? Oh no, this is just the beginning of our troubles!" she sighed. "But we're lucky; it's just a small one this time, probably just rough winds and some rain. Now would be a good time for you to show off your manly strength," she said to Doran, "carry anything on the deck down to the cabins so it doesn't get tossed off the boat."

Doran hurried to do as he was told. It was such an easy task for him to carry whatever wooden crates or heavy loads there were to move. He lifted them up effortlessly with his strong arms and carried them down quickly. His muscled body moved with ease and certainty. That's when Amara realized that she'd never really noticed how great of a Messenger Doran was until now. Minutes later, Doran came back and Amara felt a drop of rain on her head, and then it started pouring. The strong wind began pushing the still water into rising angry waves. The waves crashed against the small wooden boat and washed their faces with salty water. They slipped on the soaked deck and tried to find anything to hang on to. The mad waves continued to rock the boat and Amara feared it would tip over. She feared they would be swallowed by the furious, merciless sea and be lost in its depth forever. Every inch of her was soaked in water. The wind blew her wet hair into her face and the rain clouded her vision. She sat there or stood there, clutching tightly to who knows what. She couldn't hear herself screaming in fear and she couldn't hear the loud beats of the heart hammering against her chest over the hammering of the rain, the crashing of the waves, and the wildness of the wind. But through all that, she could still barely see the young girl with hair the color of navy, firmly holding the wheel and steering the boat surely and bravely through the storm, as though it was what she was born to do.

Chapter Twenty-One

Blinking open her eyes, Amara saw the sky clearing up. Her damp clothes were sticking to her skin and her wet hair to her face. She licked her dry lips and tasted sea salt. As she pushed herself up, she winced at the pain she felt in her right shoulder, it must have hit something during the storm. She looked around. Doran was just getting to his feet. His wet hair was flat against his face. Lavinia was sitting on the ground, panting. Her right arm was raised and the tips of her fingers were still clutching the steering wheel.

"Wow!" Doran said and gave out something between a laugh and a sigh of relief. He looked at Lavinia. "That was—that was wonderful, Lavinia. You were amazing. Thank you, you saved us!"

Lavinia looked back at him but said nothing. She looked surprised at receiving a compliment, but didn't mind.

"Yeah," Amara said, "thank you, really! That—"

Lavinia cut her off, "Stop." She turned to Amara with a look of hatred in her eyes. "Just don't. I don't want *you* to…" she trailed off. "I didn't come on this thing with you to be besties, I already told you that. I'm here for one reason and one reason only, and that's my sister. I don't like you and I certainly don't want you to like me. So, there is no point in trying to." She closed her eyes, took a deep breath in, and let it out. "Now give me the map."

Amara was a little taken aback, she just stood there.

"I don't have all day!" Lavinia shouted, "give me the stupid map and let's get on the way!"

"Fine!" Amara handed it to her.

"While I get the boat back on track, you two start emptying the deck from water," Lavinia said, "there are a couple of buckets down by the bathroom door. Make sure everything is secure and then go clean the cabins and take all the water out, they must be soaked."

Amara and Doran got to work.

Chapter Twenty-Two

They spent hours draining the boat from all the water that had come in and cleaned the cabins and whatever else Lavinia ordered them to do. When they were done, the sun was long gone and they were all exhausted. Lavinia took off to bed without a word.

"I can take tonight's shift," Doran said, trying to hide how tired he was.

"No, you took it this afternoon," said Amara, "besides, you look like you'll fall asleep standing. I can take it."

"Thanks," he smiled sleepily. "Just wake me if you get tired or need anything. Good night."

Amara took a long drink from her bottle of water. Then she took out an apple and bit into it. She stared at the two wooden mops lying on the floor. They had used them to mop the deck after getting all the water out. It brings an old memory to her head.

She was seven or eight, sitting on the floor of the woods across from her father. He held a mop in his hands and was removing the yarn from its handle. Amara copied him with the mop in her own hands.

"What are we doing, Dad?" she had asked.

"I'm going to tell you a story," he had said. Then he started speaking and capturing Amara's attention with his words like he always did. "In the past, there were some markings that existed back then but are no longer appearing now. One of those markings is the Warrior marking. We used to have a Warrior corral. They protected our land from enemies. They fought for the safety and peace of Kumilaka. Such an honorable corral they were. Do you know how the markings appear on the children of Kumilaka, Amara?" he asked his daughter.

"They just appear, don't they?"

"Not exactly, no. The markings don't just appear randomly, they choose their hosts very carefully. You see, the children drink from the water of Kumilaka and eat from its goods, right? All that enters their bodies and nourishes them comes from its land. The land learns about their desires and skills, their souls, and so it chooses the right marking for each child and presents it to them on their seventh year.

"The land can also sense and predict its own needs for the near future. So, it gives the markings that it will need to its children, and sometimes, its needs from a certain corral will not be as crucial at the time so it stops presenting the children with that marking. That is what happened to the three ancient markings. They stopped appearing. The Warrior marking is one of those markings; it had stopped appearing eighty years ago, because Kumilaka had been at peace and the war was over.

"My grandfather was a Warrior, so was his father before him. He was very proud of his corral, my granddad. He thought that our land would always need its Warriors and so he was very upset that his corral was vanishing. He trained my dad and he trained me, to fight. He also made me promise that I will teach my own children how to fight. He said you never know when you'll need to be brave and stand up to fight for your life or the lives of others.

"So," he said, standing up, "this is what we're doing today. I'm teaching you how to fight." He held up the wooden stick.

Amara had watched her father proudly as he taught her. She had wondered how he could be so brave, so strong, so smart, and so kind and caring. She looked up to her father and thought the world of him. She was the luckiest little girl, she had thought, for having the best man in the world as her father.

She didn't think that anymore. Now all she had left of her father were memories. Memories of the times he was brave and caring, memories of the times he was there. How stupid she was. It was all a fantasy. Her father had never wanted to be with them. He had never wanted to teach Amara any life lessons or sing her any songs in the forest. He had never wanted to tell her any stories before bed or carry her over his shoulders on their way to the market. He had never wanted to buy her a present every year on her birthday or comfort her with his soothing words when she was sad or hurt. He had never wanted to stick around and play with them or take care of them. He had always wanted to leave, to escape this life he had to share with them, and he did. He left.

The trapdoor on the floor of the deck swung open and out came Doran. He was soaked in sweat. His t-shirt was drenched and was sticking to his skin, wet drops of sweat were glistening against his skin and running down his face, some even looked like tears. He breathed heavily. His face was red and his eyes, his brilliant green eyes, were not smiling as they always did. They had something in them that Amara had never seen there before, fear. He looked…broken. It was the first time she had ever seen him in a short-sleeved shirt. There were bruises and scars all over his arms, covering his body as if it were a canvas and someone had been painting them on it over the years. . He seemed to have just noticed Amara. He straightened up and tried to act normal.

"Amara!" he said, his voice was tight and he stuttered with every word, "I'm sorry—I didn't mean to—I just—I—I wanted to get some air and—I'm sorry I'll go—I just…" he let his sentence trail off.

"No, no, it's okay. It's fine. You can stay. I'm just…" she turned away from him and held the steering wheel. She felt like she'd seen something she wasn't supposed to, a vulnerable side of Doran.

She heard him take a deep breath. She could see him out of the corner of her eye; he was clutching the edge of the boat and leaning down on it for support. His uncombed honey-colored hair fell over his face and he looked tired. He stood there for a few minutes, his eyes closed, forcing himself to breathe steadily. Then he stood up straight and walked down without another word.

Chapter Twenty-Three

The next morning, Lavinia came up the trapdoor early. She didn't say anything to Amara, just stood there and ate from the small bag of crackers that was in her hands. Short after, Doran came up, looking as bright and smiling as he always had.

"Good morning, girls!" he said, presenting them both with one of his bright morning smiles. Amara noticed how he briefly looked her way before turning away to the view, "What a beautiful day it is!"

"Shut it, pickle eyes!" said Lavinia, annoyed, "we talked about this. If you're planning on spreading sunshine and happiness, please do it when I'm not around. I'm sure tomato-head over here would love it, but save it for her alone, will you?"

Doran's smile was still as wide as ever.

"Oh dear, he's hopeless." Lavinia muttered.

It has been four days since they'd left Kumilaka, and they were still sailing over the deep blue. Lavinia was still an awful companion—but more so to Amara—and Doran was still his cheerful self. Amara was getting restless. Neo was back home in the hospital and she still had not reached the mountains. Lavinia said they'll arrive in two or three days. But Amara still had no idea what she was going to face when they got there. They had already faced a storm and a swarm of flying fish, and that was only on the journey to the mountains.

Right now, Doran was steering the boat and Amara was helping Lavinia gather the flying fish that ended up on deck.

"I am sick of whatever it is we're eating from home!" Lavinia had said. "It's about time we had a real meal. Now let's get these delicious beauties on a plate!" and she kept on talking about how she'll cook them.

Amara was picking up a couple of fish by her feet to put in the bucket when she saw it. The water was moving slightly, like something was stirring beneath it. She stood there and watched closely as the surface rippled and out emerged something she had never seen before.

It was big, bigger than their boat. It looked like a snake…horse…dragon? It was long and its body twisted strangely, like it hadn't a single bone in its slithering body. It towered over their boat, casted a shadow over it. It had slimy skin the color of moldy green that was filled with different sized spots in various colors, all rotten looking. There were things sprouting out of its head and floating in the air around it, it looked as though the creature had a crown made of river snakes. It had long yellow fangs growing out of its mouth and they were dripping with saliva and something that looked like blood. And it had large, greenish yellow…

"DON'T LOOK AT ITS EYES!" Lavinia yelled.

The creature was extremely close to the boat and it caused it to sway madly on the water.

"Stay with the wheel and try to keep us from tipping over!" Lavinia shouted at Doran. "Get weapons!" she ordered Amara. Amara ran down to her cabin, grabbed her bag, and flew back on deck. She flipped it over and all its contents fell out. Looking around, she saw Lavinia holding one of the mops in her hands and waving it warningly at the creature. She would have grabbed one herself but she had a feeling that the lessons her father had given her won't do her much good now.

"Be careful!" Doran shouted at Lavinia from his place by the wheel.

The creature moved closer and Lavinia struck him on the neck with the mop. Tentacles came out of nowhere and started moving madly around them. One of them flew way too close over Lavinia's head and she screamed as she ducked to the ground, the mop falling out of her hands and rolling to the other side of the boat.

"Shoot it!" Lavinia yelled, looking at the bow and arrows Amara had left on the ground.

Amara turned away from Lavinia and the creature to get them. Then she turned back to the creature, ready to shoot, and looked it right in the eyes. It was the animal from the forest, standing innocently and unknowingly in front of Amara. She looked at it and her hands shook as they held the bow and arrow pointed straight to its heart.

"SHOOT IT!" Lavinia screamed fearfully as the animal moved its hooves playfully at her. Lavinia looked at Amara with horrified eyes. "WHAT ARE YOU DOING? SHOOT IT! KILL IT, NOW!"

Amara felt her feet giving way, her face was soaked in sweat, and her heart was beating madly. She was back in the forest, the poor creature standing before her, her arrow in a perfect position to kill or wound it, but still unable to let it go. One of the animal's hooves pushed Lavinia and she let out a cry of pain as she fell back and hit something. The animal raised one of its legs above the wounded girl, getting ready to strike. The scar on Amara left brow started throbbing as she held up the bow and shot her arrow, it missed. A knife flew out of Doran's hand and shot straight into the creature's right eye. Blood splattered out of it and the ugly creature let out an ear-piercing screech as it backed away. The disgusting slimy figure lowered itself down to the water and went back from where it had emerged.

Chapter Twenty-Four

As soon as the creature was gone, Doran helped Lavinia up and sat her down near the steering wheel. Amara walked closer and she could see a rip in Lavinia's shirt and blood staining her sleeve. Doran tore the damaged sleeve off and took some stuff out of the bag that was always strapped to his back.

"What are you doing?" Lavinia winced as he put a wet cloth against her arm.

"Don't worry, I know what I'm doing," he said calmly. "My aunt was a Healer. I've seen her handle enough wounds to know what to do with this little scratch."

"Little scratch!" she said unbelievingly.

"It's okay, it's not that serious. There's no need to panic."

"Thank goodness," Amara said, standing in front of them.

Lavinia shot her head up, "What on *earth* is wrong with you?!" she yelled furiously at Amara. "That thing could have killed me! And you just stood there like a three-year-old and did nothing! I get that you hate me, and believe me, the feeling is mutual, but standing there watching me get killed, that's taking it too far! Oh, but I know why you did that, you wish me dead! You want to kill me yourself and sail this boat to the mountains without me, now that you know how to, and let my little sister die! But that sea creature came out of nowhere and was going to do your dirty business, so yay you!"

Amara stood there, appalled by what she was hearing. A burning anger was building in the pit of her stomach, an anger she had tried to control for way too long. She'd had enough. "Shut up! Shut up!" she yelled back at Lavinia, "you're the one taking this too far! I never thought any of those *monstrous* things, and it's your problem if you think everyone is as cruel and horrible as you are! It's your problem if you hate me and think I'm a terrible person, but I'm not! You did nothing but hate and torture me since as far as I can remember, and if you ask me, I'd say you're the terrible person between the two of us! It's not fair, okay? What did I ever do to you to make you hate me so much? What did I ever do to make you turn my life so miserable?"

Lavinia's face was red with anger, her fists were clenched so firmly that her knuckles turned white, and her teeth were gritted tight as if she was trying to hold back from saying something. "*You…*" she growled. "You want to know what's *not fair*?" she said through her clenched teeth. "I'LL TELL YOU WHAT'S NOT FAIR!" she started yelling, tears were welling in her eyes. "When you're six years old and the fire sirens start at night. You wake up and run out in your nightgown with your mother, and the panicked people around you say there was a fire in the Market and two people were inside when it happened. Your mom screams and you realize your father is in there. Then they say one of the men survived and the other died inside. You run in the dark to the place where the fire was being put down and see a man with dark hair being helped out of the building. You run to hug your father and see him take another little girl with burning red hair into his arms and kiss her all around as she brushes the ashes off his green hair. And you realize…" her voice cracks, "you realize that it wasn't your father who survived the fire but another girl's father. You realize as you hear your mother's screams of anguish that *your* father was lying inside in the burned down building, dead!" Lavinia's face was red and streams of tears ran down her cheeks. "That's what's *not fair*!" she spat.

Amara stared at her, in shock. She remembered the fire. She remembered how she too had run out of the house with her mother when they heard the sirens. She remembered how relief washed over her when she saw her father open his arms for her embrace. How she was so relieved that it was the other man and not her father who had died in the fire.

That was why Lavinia had hated her all these years. It wasn't her fault of course, but still. She felt bad for not giving a second thought to the other man, the man who had lost his life in the fire. The man who had a family of his own, a wife, a daughter. The man who was Lavinia's father, she hadn't thought about any of that. She was too glad that her father was alive that she didn't care about anything or anyone else.

"I'm sorry," Amara said sincerely, she wasn't sure what she was apologizing for exactly, but she felt as though she owed that to Lavinia.

Lavinia looked up at Amara and shook her head. She buried her face in her hands for a while. Then she finally raised her head and looked at Amara for a few silent moments. "Thanks," she said miserably. There was a long pause. "But it's not your fault," she forced out, "none of this is your fault. I was putting all my anger at my father's death out on you. I knew it was wrong but I—I was just so angry. I was so jealous and mad that you still had your father and I didn't."

"But I don't have my father. He's gone, he left. At least you know your father always loved you. My father abandoned me and my brother."

"Sorry," Lavinia said. And Amara was a little surprised to see her face soften slightly.

"Thanks."

And for the first time, the red-haired girl and the navy blue-haired girl smiled at each other, small but forgiving smiles.

"So, does it hurt?" Amara said apologetically, pointing at the wound on Lavinia's arm.

"Not that much," Lavinia said, "but I do wish pickle eyes here would hurry up with the bandaging." She smiled at the sight of his face.

Doran had been quietly listening to them, his hands suspended in mid-action. "Huh?" he said, realizing they were talking about him now. "Oh. Oh, yeah. I'm almost done." He nodded and went back to his work. They both laughed at him and then he joined in. The three of them sat there, laughing together under the light of the silver moon: the beginning of a new friendship.

Chapter Twenty-Five

Amara woke at the smell of food. She quickly got dressed and followed the scent up to the deck.

"Who's hungry for some real food?" Lavinia said cheerfully. Apparently, Lavinia had caught a giant fish and somehow cooked it, along with the other fish they had gathered.

"I'm starving!" Doran groaned.

"Count me in," Amara said, rubbing her eyes awake.

The fish was huge, probably the length of Amara's arm, and definitely thicker. It was freshly caught and beautifully cooked, and it filled the air around them with a brilliant smell that made Amara's empty stomach twist with desperate hunger. They've been running out of food to the point that Amara was only nibbling on the nuts and raisins she had left. It was certainly time for some real food.

The three of them sat down to eat. Amara sat on a wooden crate to keep her hands on the wheel and the other two sat on the floor. The fish Lavinia had miraculously prepared was delicious. It was so satisfying to fill one's stomach after a week of eating only old fruit and nuts. For a few minutes, there was only the sound of chewing and swallowing as they gobbled up their food gratefully.

"Lavinia, can I ask you something?" Amara said after swallowing a mouthful of fish and wiping her greasy lips.

"Yeah," Lavinia answered.

Amara hesitated for a moment before speaking, "Your dad died when you were six, so is Zuri your step-sister or something?"

Lavinia looked up from her food then back down again, "I was an only child before, just me, my mom, and my dad," she explained, "about two years after my dad died, my mom remarried. The man she married," Amara could tell by the way Lavinia mentioned him that she wasn't his biggest fan, "he had four boys from his first wife. So, out of nowhere, I had four stepbrothers."

"Wow," Amara proclaimed, "that must have been hard."

Lavinia gave out a short laugh. "You can bet on that. They can be incredibly awful when they want. The two that are older than me barely acknowledge my existence, and the twins—they're a year younger than me—have a mission of making my life as dreadful as they can manage." She sighed loudly and took a bite off her plate. She chewed for a few seconds and a small smile appeared on her face, "Then came Zuri, she's my half-sister," Lavinia explained, "I love that little girl." She shook her head and smiled fondly. "She always followed me around and bragged about me in school. She's just…the best. I can't lose her; she's the only light in my life."

Amara nodded and gave a sad smile. "Yeah, I know what you mean. Neo is the only light in my life, everyone else is gone. My mother died giving birth to him. I was seven." She shrugged.

"When did your dad leave?" Lavinia questioned.

"He left a year after my mom died. Never said why. He just left his daughter and one-year-old son with his sister and took off. Best father-of-the-year award goes to him, I guess." Amara joked in an attempt to lighten the mood.

Lavinia's mouth formed half a smile. "What happened then?"

"Well, we lived with my Aunt Kaila for two years and a half. She died in an accident when I was eleven, and just like that, we were all alone. They sent us to the Children's Home after that and we've been there ever since."

"That must have been real tough for you guys," Lavinia said sympathetically, and Amara nodded.

There was a moment's silence, where they all stared at their food. Then Lavinia spoke.

"What about you?" she turned to Doran, who had been sitting there silently all this time, listening to them. He seemed to be doing that a lot. "What's the story of your life?" she asked dramatically.

Doran blinked at her for a few seconds before clearing his throat loudly. "What? I don't know, really."

"Do you have any siblings?" Lavinia asked after thinking for a moment.

"Uh," Doran said, a bit taken aback, "no, I—I don't. I wish I did though," he added, considering it as he took a drink of water from his bottle. He placed it back on the floor and continued, "Both my parents died when I was too little to remember. I don't know anything about them." He shrugged.

"I didn't know that," Amara said, a little surprised and disappointed with herself for not realizing Doran was an orphan (somewhat like her) in all the years she worked with him. "I'm sorry."

"It's alright," he smiled, "I wasn't entirely on my own, I lived with my uncle and his wife since I was a kid. It wasn't the best life," he admitted, "but I got used to it."

"Your aunt's the one who was a Healer, right?" Lavinia questioned.

"Yeah," Doran nodded, a little surprised she remembered that, "my aunt was a Healer and my uncle's a Laborer." Doran stopped talking for a moment then said, "He never liked me really. He had the worst temper and always got mad at me. My aunt was great though, she treated me like her son. But when she died, it was awful. My uncle hated me more than ever, he was always furious, and he lost his temper and raged at me whenever I did anything he didn't like." Amara thought she saw him wince. "Or if he was just in a bad mood." A hint of disgust laced his last words.

"I just wanted to leave, to run away. I even tried it once." He gave a half-hearted laugh. "He almost killed me when he found out…" He stopped talking suddenly, seeming to realize what he was saying. He looked up with an alarmed look on his face, like he said something he wasn't supposed to. "I'm sorry. I didn't mean to say all that. I shouldn't have rambled on. I just—"

"It's okay, Doran," Amara said with an assuring smile.

"Yeah," Lavinia said, "apparently, we're all spilling out our darkest secrets today," she laughed, took a last bite off her now plate, and sat back.

Doran smiled a nervous smile back at them. "I just never told anyone that much about myself."

"Well, I'm glad you told us," Amara said.

"Yes, such an honor," Lavinia added solemnly, "I am flattered."

Three children who have all faced loss and pain in their lives, sat there sharing food, secrets, and tragic pasts. They were sailing together towards the unknown, but there was one thing they now knew, that they were no longer alone.

Chapter Twenty-Six

They were almost there. So close. Amara could see the mountains from a distance. Lavinia was steering the boat and Amara stood with Doran looking at the mountains from afar.

The closer they got, the worst Amara felt. She was nervous, so nervous, so scared. What if she failed? What if she didn't manage to get the cure? What then? All she was thinking of this whole time was getting here. She said she'd have time to figure out what to do and how to get the cure when she got there. Now she was almost here and had no clue what she was going to do. Neo was waiting for her to come back. What if she didn't make it back?

"What's wrong?" Doran asked when he saw the troubled look on her face.

"What am I going to do?" she said in a tight voice. She was clutching her stomach because it was beginning to ache from nervousness and her hands were shaking in panic. "I don't know how to do this. How can I possibly get the cure? What if it isn't even there? Neo is waiting for me! I promised him I'll come back! How can I promise him something like that? What if I die? I don't know what's going to happen! I don't know how to do this!"

"Hey, hey, hey," Doran said, trying to calm her down. He looked her in the eyes and talked calmly and convincingly, "You'll be okay. You are going to get that cure and you are not going to die. I'll make sure of that. You can do it, Amara, I know you can." He smiled at her. It was a gentle and reassuring smile. His green eyes looked at her with nothing but truth in them. "You are going to make it back to your brother. I believe in you."

She nodded, gaining some confidence from Doran's words.

"Amara, can I ask you something?" he said, moments later.

"Yeah, sure."

"Why do you cover up your marking?"

Out of habit, her hand flew up to her forehead and she batted her bangs down to make sure it was covered. She didn't answer.

"I think it's beautiful, it's the prettiest marking I've ever seen, and it's unique. I don't think you should be ashamed of it. I think you should be proud of it, Mara."

Amara turned to him.

"What?" he asked after she stared at him for a moment too long.

"Nothing, it's just…no one except Elianah and my mother has ever called me Mara."

"Oh, I'm sorry. If you don't want me to, I—"

"No, it's okay. I like it," she smiled at him.

He smiled back, his happy and good-natured smile.

"I see a piece of land close by," Lavinia called to them, "I think we should stop there to get some supplies. Maybe spend the night? Then we'll head straight to the mountains."

Chapter Twenty-Seven

When they landed on the shore and tied up their boat, there was a place that could be seen from far away. Smoke was coming out of its chimney. It looked like an old inn. "Okay," Amara said, "it's getting dark. We can go in there and warm up. Then get a room for the night and head out tomorrow."

"Sounds good," Doran said.

They started walking and by the time they reached the inn, it was pitch black. "It looks like we can get some water from out here," Lavinia said, pointing at something a few feet away.

"Oh yeah, let's go get some," said Doran.

Amara wasn't paying attention, she wanted to get inside. "How about I go in and get us rooms while you pick up the water," she said.

"Sure," Lavinia said, already walking away.

"Be careful, don't get lost," Doran said before turning away.

Amara went inside, escaping the darkness. She walked in and stood by the door as it closed behind her. She took a look around, examining the place. It was small, lit dimly by the candles hanging on the walls, but still very noisy. It was filled with the buzz of talking people and clanking of plates and dishes. There was a set of stairs in the corner that Amara assumed lead to the rooms. Wooden tables and stools filled the place and it looked as though they tried to cram as much of them into the small room as possible, which made it very crowded. There were a bunch of people around that all looked like they came from different places. They sat eating on the tables or drinking and laughing on the stools…

Amara's heart fell to her stomach. Her body went cold and rigid. Her hands shook at her sides. She stood there, unbelieving. She felt her feet turned to jelly. Her hands frantically searched for the doorknob. She needed to go out, to escape this impossible dream. She opened the door and flung herself out into the darkness.

A man inside glimpsed a wave of red hair flying out the door.

Chapter Twenty-Eight

Amara stood outside, panting. She felt like crying, she felt like yelling, she felt like vomiting. But she felt unable to do any of that. At first, she'd thought her eyes were playing tricks on her. But then she saw that laugh, the laugh she knew too well. How his head fell back as he let out that roar of laughter. He sat there, laughing, like he didn't have a care in the world. Her stomach turned.

Someone let out a yell in the distance but it was quickly muffled. Amara's head shot up, Lavinia! She ran towards the source of the sound but it was way too dark to see anything.

"Get off!" Lavinia's voice yelled in the dark.

"Shut up!" a gruff stranger's voice said, and her yells were muffled once more.

"Let her go, now!" Doran growled, "I told you we don't have anything!" There was clear panic in his voice. He was struggling against someone.

"Doran, where are you?!" Amara shouted into the night, her voice came out shaky. Unable to see anything, she held her hands in front of her, feeling her way.

Someone grabbed her from the back, she yelled but he quickly put his hand over her mouth.

"GET YOUR FILTHY HANDS OFF OF HER!" Doran yelled, and his voice was dangerous.

A punch. A groan.

"I'm gonna show you, boy!" another stranger said, his voice was rough. A loud punch. A cry of pain. Doran! Amara wanted to run to him. She struggled against the tall figure holding her back. He smelled of cigarettes and another foul odor. Amara heard something smash and the man holding her fell to the floor with a yell. Someone had hit him on the head. She ran towards Doran, or Lavinia, she didn't know exactly. She thought she heard Lavinia kicking someone. But someone had tried to pull her back from the neck of her shirt and she tumbled to the ground, hitting her head on the cold stone floor. There were circles dancing around her. The world was spinning. Someone hit someone. Someone fell to the ground. Someone got punched. Someone yelled. It was a blur of loud noises and movements in the dark. Then there was the sound of a door slamming open and a series of loud shouts.

After that, someone slowly lifted her into their arms and carried her up. She drifted into a darker darkness.

Chapter Twenty-Nine

Darkness. Silence. Unidentifiable voices in the darkness. Doran's voice. Someone else's voice. *No.*

Amara raised herself up quickly. Her head spun, her vision was blurred. Someone rushed to her side and put her down on the bed again. The world slowly came into focus. A figure was crouched over her. A pair of eyes, big ocean blue eyes: her eyes. She let out a small scream and jumped out of the bed. She stared at the man before her. It was him.

A tall figure with broad shoulders and strong arms stood in the room. He had a diamond-shaped face and a sharp chin. He had thin lips and thick dark brows. But most noticeable of all was his messy dark green hair that had grown long, and his wide ocean blue eyes: Her father.

"Amara," he said with his warm voice, the voice she hadn't heard in years. It made a shiver run down her spine. He wore shabby clothes. His dark green hair was clearly unwashed, for weeks probably, and it had grown longer than she'd ever seen it. He looked thinner than she remembered him. His figure still looked broad and strong like always, but he somehow looked smaller and weaker, broken somehow. She might be imagining it, but she could almost smell the faint scent of liquor pouring out from him. He did look somewhat steady now. He wasn't swaying as bad as she'd seen him do before and his expression was alert, as though someone had slapped him awake from a long dream. But she could still sniff out the nasty sweet and chemical odor. The smell seemed to be coming from his breath and sweat and it reminded Amara of the awful nights she'd tried so hard to forget. Now he was reaching his hands gently towards her.

"GO AWAY!" she screamed. "DON'T COME NEAR ME!"

Doran took a step toward her protectively. Her father stopped. She stared at him; her mind still unable to comprehend the truth. Her father was here. Her father, who she had not seen in six full years, was now standing before her. "Amara, sweetie, it's me. Calm down and let's talk," he said pleadingly.

"NO!" Amara found herself yelling at him. She had never raised her voice at her father like that. All those years, she fantasized about him coming back. She dreamed about this moment, when her father finally stood in front of her. She was going to run into his arms and tell him how much she had missed him. But right now, all she could feel was hurt and anger rising uncontrollably to the surface. All the anger she had felt towards him in the past six years came rushing back at this moment. "You want to talk? I'll talk!" she spat poisonously. "You LEFT! You left us all alone! It wasn't enough that Mom had died, you had to take off! You never even wanted to stay! You couldn't wait to run away!" She pointed a finger accusingly at him. "All those times you laughed with us and told us stories and told us you loved us; those were all LIES! You left us! You left us all ALONE!" Her whole body was shaking now and she was crying hysterically, tears of anger, tears of sorrow.

She saw something in her father's eyes. It looked like hurt. But he had no right to be upset. He was the one who'd hurt them.

"That is not true!" he said, his voice a little defensive. "I—I didn't leave you all alone. I left you with your Aunt Kaila. I was a mess at the time and she could take care of you better than me and—"

"Aunt Kaila is dead!" Amara shouted at him. Maybe a bit too harshly, considering she was his sister. But she didn't care at the moment. Something washed over her father's face. Some small part of her wanted to go hug him tight like she used to do when he came home from work, tired or upset. But she was so mad at him right now that she couldn't.

"I—I didn't know," he said, his voice was croaky.

"Of course you didn't know," Amara sobbed uncontrollably, "you left! You left and Aunt Kaila died and we were all alone! I had to take care of Neo all by myself! I was eleven! I wasn't supposed to take care of him, and Aunt Kaila wasn't supposed to take care of us. That was your job!"

"Amara I was—I was so sad after your mom died that I just—I couldn't stay and take care of you kids. I couldn't do it without her. I—I couldn't take care of myself without her!" he was crying now.

A memory forced itself into her mind…

It was after her mom had died. Amara was lying in bed at night, wide-awake. She was supposed to go to sleep but she couldn't bring herself to. It was hard to sleep ever since her mom died. She was used to having her mother sing to her before bed, or her father tell her a story. So, she decided to get up and ask him to do that. She walked out of her room and peeked into the living room. That's when she saw it. Her father was standing in the middle of the room. He wasn't standing very well though. His feet were swaying left and right and he tried to hold on to the wall for balance. Out of nowhere, he started yelling. Screaming as loud as his lungs would allow. His yells drowned out her baby brother's crying from the other room. Amara was frozen in place. She had never seen her father like this. He screamed and sobbed and kicked and threw anything he could get his hands on. He picked up things from around the room and smashed them on the floor and against the walls. He hit and punched the walls with all the power he could muster until his knuckles started bleeding. He kicked the tables and doors until his feet started throbbing. He screamed and yelled and shouted and cried and sobbed until his head was throbbing too. Amara slowly walked into the room.

"Daddy!" she said loudly to be heard, tears in her voice.

Her father turned when he heard her. But when he looked at her, she saw something dangerous in his eyes. Her father had never looked at her that way. She'd never forget that look on his face. It was as if she could see his soul burning through his eyes. There was so much pain and anger in there. They were wild and scary. And as he looked at her like that, it was as if he didn't recognize her. He picked up one of the empty glass bottles lying on the ground and yelled as he smashed it hard against the wall behind Amara. She screamed in fear and crouched down covering her head with her arms. That's when the door to the house opened and her Aunt Kaila ran in. She quickly ran to Amara to check if she was alright, as her father stared at her unbelievingly. His eyes looked at her fearfully; he shook his head desperately as if he couldn't believe what he had just done. The rest of the night was a blur. Except for the whispers she'd heard when she lay on her bed later on.

"What were you thinking?" that was her Aunt Kaila. She was whisper yelling at her brother. "You could've hurt them! This is not acceptable; do you understand me? This has to stop! This has to stop before one of your kids gets badly hurt!"

Her father's response was slow, his words slurred and senseless. "This has to stop," he repeated the words, "this has to stop."

Now, still sobbing, she looked at her father, who looked back at her with sad eyes.

"I was scared," he said in a small voice, he sounded like a little kid. His voice was pleading, begging for her to understand. "I was so sad and so scared."

"You shouldn't have left," Amara said, shaking her head, no longer yelling. Her voice was a little above a whisper. She was looking at him with a look of disdain, but there was no trace of pity in her eyes. "Neo has been touched. That's why we're here. We want to get the cure."

She turned around and left the room before she could see the look on his face. He had a right to know, but he had no right to look sad in front of her.

Chapter Thirty

Amara was eight. Aunt Kaila was at their house like she had been very often recently. Her father called her outside, and he had a bag over his shoulders. Amara thought they were going together to the forest or to town. She was excited; they haven't done that in a while.

"Amara, sweetheart, I have to tell you something," he said.

"What is it, Dad?" she asked.

He got down on his knee and put one arm on her shoulder. "I have to go somewhere for a while," he said.

"Go somewhere, where?" she asked curiously.

"Somewhere far away."

"Like on a trip? Will Neo come?"

"Oh no, honey. Neo can't come."

"So, he's staying with Aunt Kaila? I think he'd like to come with us. Maybe Neo and Aunt Kaila can both come. That'll be nice."

Her father looked at her sadly. "Sweetie, I'm going by myself. You and your brother are both staying here with Aunt Kaila."

"What? No! I'm coming with you," she said.

He shook his head. "No, Amara. You're staying here."

"Why? Why are you leaving? And why can't I come?"

"I just—I have to go away for a while Amara. I have to go alone. I'm sorry. I really don't want to leave you and your brother but I—I have to."

"But—but—when are you leaving?"

"Now, sweetheart. I'm leaving now."

"*What?* When are you coming back?"

"I—I don't know when I'm coming back."

"NO! I'm not gonna let you go! You can't go, not without me."

"I'm sorry, honey, I have to," his voice cracked.

"Don't leave me alone!" she cried.

"No, no. I'm not leaving you alone. Your Aunt Kaila will be here, and she'll take good care of you two, I promise." He put his hand over her head and stroked her red hair.

"But I want you, Dad! I want you to stay."

"I'm sorry, sweetie, I have to go. Believe me, I don't want to, and it hurts me to go but I really need to."

"Then don't go! Don't go!" she said desperately.

He leaned down to kiss her. "I love you, kid. I love you more than anything, remember that."

"NO!"

He hugged her tight but she struggled against him. "NO, NO, NO!" she sobbed as she hit his chest with her small fists, and he tried his hardest to hold back his own tears.

"Honey, I'm sorry. I'm so, so sorry that I have to do this," he said, trying to hold down her hands.

She calmed down for a second. "When are you coming back?" she asked, not bothering to wipe the tears streaming down her face.

"I don't know, love," he said, wiping the drops off her pretty face.

"But you are coming back, right?" she asked fearfully.

"Yes, honey, I am."

"You promise?"

He was silent for a moment. "I promise," he said wearily, his eyes were tired, so tired. He sat there for another minute, looking at his daughter. Then he stood up. "I have to go now," he said.

"NO!" Amara crumpled the tip of his shirt in her hands and held it tightly. "Don't go, please. Please don't go, Dad. I'll be good. I'll do anything you want. Just don't go. Please. Please," she begged and sobbed.

"I'm sorry," her father said weakly, his voice was strangled. He opened his mouth to say something but his voice caught in his throat as his eyes started swarming with tears.

Then he pulled her off of him and walked away. He didn't look back.

"NO! DAD! COME BACK!" she yelled after him. "PLEASE! DON'T GO! DAD, COME BACK!"

She yelled and cried and screamed and ran to try and follow her father but her Aunt Kaila held her back. She took the little girl back into the house as she struggled madly to free herself and go after him.

When Amara barged out of the room, Doran followed her.

"Mara, are you okay?" he asked concernedly, stepping in her way.

"Yes. I just…" she covered her face in her hands for a few seconds. "I'm fine," she finally said, lifting her head. "We have to start moving. So just get Lavinia and all our stuff and let's get going."

He looked at her for a moment before answering back. "Okay. I'll get Lavinia and we'll be on our way."

He walked away, and that's when Amara realized they were inside someone's home. She looked around and saw many frames hanging on the mustard yellow walls. The frames held pictures of people at different stages of their lives. They smiled happily at Amara. There were several doors in the hallway she stood in, identical brown wooden doors with big brass knobs. The walls and doors were scratched at certain spots, apparently from age. Amara hurried down the short flight of stairs into a cozy room with a big red couch. In front of the couch were a small wooden table and a couple of mismatched chairs. There were picture frames filling this room too, along with a lot of trinkets and knick-knacks lying everywhere. This room had the same mustard yellow wallpaper as the hallway upstairs and was decorated with several flower vases. In fact, the entire room was decorated with flowers. The teal curtains had a floral pattern on them and looked as if they were hand-knitted. The blankets and pillows thrown on the couch were no different. The whole place smelled like freshly picked lilies, peach pies, all types of berries, and home-cooked meals.

Someone walked into the room. It was a plump-looking woman with faded auburn hair and hazel eyes. She wore an old-fashioned dress with the same floral pattern on the curtains and her hair was pulled back into a neat bun. She was holding a tray in her hands and it held a basket of bread and a plate of fruit.

"Oh, hello dear," the woman said in a fruity voice when she saw Amara, "I see you've woken up. So, how are you feeling?" She smiled at Amara. Her smile was warm and welcoming and it somehow unknotted one of the million knots in Amara's chest. But Amara was still looking at her in confusion. Why were they in this strange lady's house? The woman looked at Amara's confused face and gave a little warm-hearted laugh. "I'm so sorry, I forgot to introduce myself," she said. Then she held out her hand. "I'm Agatha."

Amara shook her hand. "I'm Amara," she said, a little unsurely.

"Nice to meet you, my dear," said Agatha as she smiled sincerely. "Now, sit down and eat, I'm sure your friends are coming down soon." She pushed Amara down to sit on the comfy couch. She went back through the door she came in – which Amara presumed led to the kitchen – and came back with another tray, this one held a pot of tea and a few different sized mugs. She poured them both a mug of tea.

"I was making myself some tea to sit down and read last night when I heard them," Agatha said, "I walked out and saw those horrid men fighting your friends on the street and you poor thing lying there on the ground. I sure showed them though. No one fights on my lawn. Trust me; all men are afraid of old ladies with slippers to hit with. They ran away like the rats they are," she laughed heartily.

CHAPTER THIRTY-ONE

Lavinia, Doran, and Amara thanked the lady for her help and hospitality before they left. Doran had even offered his manly services. He ended up fixing some of the broken things around the lady's house, which certainly made her fill up with joy. She insisted on packing them some food for the journey.

"Don't you thank me, dears, it was no trouble at all," Agatha said, "it was great to have some company in this empty house for a change, trust me. And I can't tell you how much I appreciated your help, my dear." She pinched Doran's cheek affectionately and his face broke into a shy smile. "If you ever need a place to stay, please don't hesitate in visiting. You are always welcome here."

They walked around the small village and gathered up some of the things they'll need for the journey home with the very little money they had. After they got everything, they needed to get ready for the trip, they asked someone from the village about the mountains, and he told them the best way to get there. He also added some nonsense that Amara decided to ignore, hoping that he at least gave them the right directions.

"It isn't that far," the old man said, he had a thick accent. "It is a little over a five hour's journey from here. But remember that the Emberose Mountains will not welcome you unless you pass. Most never pass. They say no one but one passes. But you have to—"

"Yes. Yes, we got it, thank you," Lavinia interrupted him a bit rudely. The old man looked up at them. He was wearing an old and worn cloak and had his head covered with a hood. But when he raised his head, Amara could see his bearded face and black eyes. She hoped they hadn't offended him.

They thanked him and then headed on their way back to the boat.

Amara walked at the front, Doran and Lavinia following her. She was still thinking about what happened this morning and she didn't want to deal with the other two's worried looks and careful questions.

"Do you think we packed enough water?" Lavinia asked Doran behind her.

"Yeah, I think it'll be quite enough," he said, "to be honest, I'm a little worried about the food we packed. Don't you think packing all that jam is going to attract wild animals of some sort?" he asked unsurely.

"You are so stupid!" Lavinia said, a laugh in her voice.

"What? I was just wondering!"

"Wait! Wait!" someone called from close behind them.

"What does *he* want?" Lavinia said, and Amara could feel her giving one of her dangerous looks. Amara's father was hurrying after them.

"I'm coming with you," he said, a little out of breath.

"No, you're not," Amara said without looking at him. "Let's go, we want to set sail before dark." They went on walking but her father followed.

"Stop it!" Amara shouted, still not turning around. "Go away! We don't want your company, thank you very much. It's a little too late."

"Well, I don't care what you want, I'm coming," he said, walking behind them. "I've been out hunting all my life and went on trips like these before so I'll be a lot of help." He took a small breath and let it out. "Amara, I know you're very mad at me right now, and I know I deserve it. But even if I haven't been much of a father for you and Neo these past few years, I still am your father. And just like you said, it's my job to take care of you guys, whether you like it or not. My little boy is sick and I'm coming with you to help save him, and I'm not about to let my little girl go on this by herself."

"I am not your little girl," she said angrily, "I haven't been that for a while now." She walked on and was glad to hear her father's steps still behind her. She was still furious at him of course, but at least this time, he was sticking around.

They walked for a while of Amara ignoring her father, Lavinia shooting him untrusting looks, and Doran staying close to him as though he suspected he would grab Amara and run away. Then they reached the boat and it didn't look like Amara's father was planning on letting them go without him. After sailing for a few hours, they all sat on the deck to eat. Doran was sailing the boat and they all sat on the ground around him. Lavinia passed some nuts to Amara and Doran and deliberately skipped Amara's father.

"Uh so," Doran said, approaching Amara's father cautiously and trying to start a conversation, "what was your corral back in Kumilaka—err—sir?" he added unsurely.

"You can call me Kellan," he said, "Hunter Kellan. I love hunting. Being in the arms of the forest and the peace and quiet of nature, there's nothing quite like it."

Amara noticed her father was looking at Lavinia, and she had a feeling it wasn't because of the nuts.

"Are you—are you Kwan's daughter?" he asked suddenly, his head tilted to one side and his brow furrowed.

Lavinia's head shot up. "What?" she said.

"Are you Fisher Kwan's daughter?" he asked again.

"Yes," she said slowly. Her eyes were narrowed at him.

Kellan smiled. "I thought so. You look a lot like him."

"You knew my dad?" Lavinia asked. Her gaze was steady.

"Yes, I did. Almost everyone knew Kwan. He was a great man. I mean, we weren't the closest friends," he gave a small smile, "we were best friends at school actually, but after getting marked, we went our separate ways and didn't see that much of each other anymore. We did see each other every once and a while though, and it was like no time had passed at all." The smile slowly faded from his face. He looked up at Lavinia, "He saved me, you know, the night of the fire."

Lavinia took in a sharp breath but still didn't take her eyes off of him.

"I was…" he took a deep breath and he stared at something in the far distance. "I was trapped and couldn't get out. He could've escaped the fire but he came back for me. He came back and saved me. But then more wood fell from the ceiling and it was over for him. He told me to leave. His last words were 'Tell them I love them; tell my baby I love her more than anything," he was whispering now. His eyes were glassy, like he was seeing something none of them could. "I did. I told your mom what happened and what he said. She didn't let me speak to you though; she said you were too little to understand." He looked at Lavinia again, "I'm telling you now. Your father loved you. Your father loved you more than anything. He didn't mean to leave you." For a second, Amara felt as though he was talking to her. "He was a hero and a good friend. The bravest and kindest man I ever knew."

Lavinia was looking at him with teary eyes. She nodded. "He was." Amara expected her voice to break, but it didn't. It was full with pride and sadness and love. "Thank you."

She then passed him the bag of nuts.

Chapter Thirty-Two

They were here, in the Mountains of Emberose. They stood on the rocky shore, taking in all the glorious colors blending together before their eyes. The sun was setting above the horizon, casting a dreamlike glow that painted the endless sky with the brightest shade of orange. Birds were flying above them like shadows, black wings against the peach sky. Blue waves crashing gently against sharp gray rocks. The cool breeze carried a spray of salty water and tickled their cheeks as it danced gracefully around them. Somewhere in here was the cure for the Touch. They were so close, so close to getting it, so close to going home. After walking for what felt like an hour, they reached an opening in one of the mountains. The four of them stood before a huge cave mouth and Amara knew that was where they were supposed to go.

"We're going in," she said.

"Are you sure?" Lavinia said, "it's dark in there."

Amara hesitated.

"We have torches," Doran said. He took some out of the bag that he was weirdly attached to and passed them around.

"Okay. Then I guess we're set," Kellan said, "let's go in." He walked inside and they followed him in.

The floor was littered with small and sharp rocks and the ceiling was a hundred feet high, hanging from it were a thousand stalactites and sleeping bats. It was dim and chilly. The only sounds that could be heard were the echoing footsteps of four pairs of feet and the dripping of water in a distance.

"Where do you think it leads?" Doran asked quietly.

"I have no clue," Amara said with a voice quieter than his.

They were whispering for some reason, like they didn't want to disturb the quietness of this abandoned place. Like sound was something foreign and unwelcome in here. Like they were trespassers on this ancient property, and maybe they were. For a while, nothing happened. Amara had no idea of how long they had walked or how deep they were into the cave. They were walking in silence. Only giving short comments and brief responses every once in a while. The sound of their footsteps on the hard and wet cave floor was echoing in Amara's head like it was on replay. At some point, Amara noticed another sound in the quiet of the cave. She wasn't sure for how long exactly it had been there. It was a very low rumbling sound. It vibrated rhythmically in the air and sounded like heavy breathing or growling, or both. Just as Amara was trying to identify the source of the sound, they all heard a loud thumping echoing through the walls. They could also feel the ground vibrating beneath their feet.

"What the—?" Lavinia started, but she was cut off by the giant figure that had come out of nowhere. It was horrendous, ten feet of skin and hair. It was standing on its hind legs and had a very arched back that made it look as though it had twisted its bones to look that way. The entire body of the creature was covered in rough long hair that was in different shades of black and brown. The hair was insanely tangled and was dirty with twigs and saliva and bugs and who knows what else. There were patches where there was no hair and you could see the ugly skin beneath. Sticking out from the head to the lower back were small white horns that looked like they could crack open a nutshell with no effort. Its face was sprouting with filthy brown hair, but you could still manage to see the big mouth that had the yellowest and most crooked teeth ever. Each tooth sprang out in a different direction, but they were all as sharp as knives. The eyes were dead black and somehow forced a chill to go through every inch of bone you had when you looked at them. That was what happened to Amara when she stared with horror at the beast standing before their four tiny figures. The ghastly being looked around at its surroundings before spotting them. Its eyes went even darker and scarier, if that was possible. They glinted as he caught sight of his fresh new meal. A greedy sort of growl escaped the beast's mouth as it started toward them.

"RUN!" Amara yelled and they all sprung away in the other direction, running with all their might. The beast followed. It was a bit slow, feet thumping heavily on the stone floor and making the earth shake around them. But it was huge and was bound to catch up to them eventually. Then it'll probably kill them on the spot.

"The only way to escape it is to go back out the cave," Doran said, sounding not as out of breath as he should have been.

"But what about the cure?" Lavinia asked anxiously.

"We can't leave the cave," Amara said, "we have to get through it and keep going."

"Get through it?" Lavinia asked loudly.

"Yes," said Amara a little unsurely.

"If we get anywhere closer to that thing, it'll tear us apart to pieces and gobble us up for dinner," Lavinia said.

"We might have a chance," said Kellan. That's when the beast jumped into view and gave a loud growl that made them all jump. Kellan stepped in front of all of them and spread his hands wide at his sides as if to shield the others from view. "Get back, all of you!" he shouted at them. Out from under his jacket, he pulled a rusty-looking dagger and held it firmly in his hands as he circled the beast.

The beast's gleaming black eyes were staring intensely at Kellan. It looked as though it had forgotten the other three were even there. Kellan was staring right back at him, careful not to blink. If he was scared or nervous, it certainly did not show. He looked as sure as someone could ever be while staring at a ten-feet-tall monster with nothing but a battered dagger in hand. Kellan moved slowly and carefully but he looked like a wild animal himself, ready to pounce. The beast growled steadily and clenched its yellow teeth at Kellan as drool ran from its mouth and down its hairy chin. Suddenly, it swung its giant arm and Amara screamed. But Kellan was too quick; he ducked out of its way and dug the dagger into the beast's outstretched arm. A ground-shaking yell escaped the giant's mouth and Kellan stepped out of its way as it thrashed its enormous fists against the floor furiously. The beast looked at Kellan with merciless eyes and started walking toward him, thumping its feet hurriedly. It looked like Kellan wouldn't be able to escape it this time.

"Give me something," he called back to them. But the beast had almost reached him, they couldn't be that quick. In a matter of seconds, Doran grabbed Amara's bag, slid out the bow and arrows, ran as quick as lightning, and threw them to Kellan. He did all that in such a smooth manner that made it seem as though he had practiced these movements a hundred times before. Kellan caught them right away and quickly adjusted them, bow held tight in hand and arrow poised perfectly. Without a moment's hesitation, the sharp arrow flew out of the Hunter's hands and straight into the beast's heart. The giant hairy thing let out an earsplitting scream before tumbling to the floor and falling with the loudest thud.

Amara let out a gasp of horror or relief, or maybe both. The beast's lifeless body lay on the floor of the cave, where a giant pool of blood was forming. Amara had a small urge to run out of here and throw up all the contents in her uneasy stomach. But she turned her eyes away from the dead figure of the beast on the floor and swallowed that down.

"Thanks for that, kid," Kellan said to Doran and gave him a friendly slap on the back. "You've got a pretty slick way, haven't you? A Messenger?"

Doran nodded.

"Not bad," Kellan said and then turned to all of them, "follow me."

They passed the bloody corpse without another glance.

CHAPTER THIRTY-THREE

The four of them walked for what felt like hours, until their feet started to ache. Amara was sure that when she pulled her shoes off, she'd find blisters. But she didn't really care; sore feet were the least of her concerns at the moment. She stared at the rocky surfaces as she kept on walking, and tried to focus on nothing but the sharp edges of rocks and the cracks on the walls. She pushed all the other frightening thoughts out of her head. Her mind was completely blank now except for the sounds of their echoing footsteps and the dim colors she saw on the walls. Black. Gray. Black. Gray. Black. Green. They were beginning to see greenish roots sprouting out of the cold stonewalls. Suddenly, out of nowhere, came a thick, snake-like green stem. It stabbed the air in front of them like a sword, wanting to kill. Then it hovered up there for a moment and they all stared at it in horror. On the green skin of the plant were sharp thorns that had a yellow liquid oozing out of them. Another one of the moving plants flew out of nowhere and almost hit Kellan's arm, but he pulled back at the last second.

"Watch out!" he shouted. "I think they might be poisonous. *Don't* let them touch you!"

Whoosh. Amara heard it coming from her left and jumped away in an instant. Lavinia ducked as one of them flew in her direction. Doran took a knife out of his pocket and threw it to Amara. She held it firmly in her hands, ready to defend herself. They walked slowly, carefully glancing around them for any poisonous plants. Occasionally, one of them would fly out in an attempt to attack but they'd be ready for it. Each one of them was watchful, their eyes darting all around them.

Then Amara saw it. From very far away, she saw the tiny doorway in a distance. Inside it was a glow of faint gold that cast small beams of light on the rocky floor of the cave. She stopped walking suddenly and stared at it.

"That's it," she whispered to herself. Inside that doorway was the cure. The cure she needed to save her brother.

"Mara!" Someone shoved her and knocked her hard to the floor. Amara fell on the cold stone floor with a shock and gasped as the impact knocked the air out of her lungs. She felt the tip of something sharp and rigid cut her cheek. Then she opened her eyes and waited for them to focus, and shook her head to clear the black spots dancing around her. When she glanced up, she saw Doran on his knees by her side, the killer plant hovering over him. It slowly slithered back into its hiding place. Amara stared at the scene in front of her, slowly taking it in.

"You saved me," she said, out of breath. Doran looked up at her and let out a breath of relief. He smiled: gentle and radiant.

"You saved me!" she said incredulously, "are you insane? Why would you do something like that?" He looked slightly taken aback. She got up – ignoring the fact that she was a little out of balance – and walked over to him, pointing a finger in his direction and shouting accusingly. "You could've hurt yourself! You could've seriously hurt yourself! And who gave you the right to save me? Who gave you the right to risk your own life to save my neck, huh? Are you okay? Did it hurt you?" she asked, not any less furious. She started examining him for any wounds.

"I'm fine!" he said, shaking her off. "Calm down, okay?" He smiled at her softly. "I'm fine. Are you?" he frowned and his brow furrowed as he looked at her. He reached out to touch her cheek. "I hurt you."

Amara pulled away quickly and put her finger on the cut. "No, you didn't. It's just a scratch." She looked at him. "Don't you ever do that again," she said warningly and smacked his shoulder, "but, thank you."

"Are you okay, honey?" her father said, hurrying toward her, looking worried. She nodded and walked away. He turned to Doran and thanked him quietly.

"You think we should go in there?" Lavinia pointed at the faraway door.

"Yeah," Amara said.

"Then let's get going," Doran said, walking behind them.

"Let's get going," Amara repeated, taking a deep breath.

They went on their way.

Chapter Thirty-Four

They walked for a long time but Amara thought the door didn't seem to be getting any closer. It was still a tiny slit in the distance, golden light escaping through it and lighting up the surrounding darkness. Amara let out a disgruntled sound. She was getting restless again.

"We're almost there," Kellan said, in what sounded like a reassuring voice.

"No, we're not," she said angrily, turning to look at them but not stopping. Kellan and Lavinia were walking behind her and Doran was further back. "Why are you all walking so slow? Will you please hurry up already? We're not taking a walk!" Doran looked up from the ground and picked up his pace a bit. She rolled her eyes at them and walked ahead.

She was thinking of Neo. What was he doing now? Was he still waiting for her? Was he okay? Or was she too late? No. No. No. She must not think that way. She must not think at all. Just clear her head and focus on the path ahead. Amara forced the thoughts out of her head. She caught Lavinia and Kellan's low voices from behind.

"…and how is she doing back home?" Kellan asked in a voice barely louder than a whisper. Amara had to listen hard to hear them.

"I don't really know," Lavinia said, "we weren't the best of friends back home, to be honest." This was the biggest understatement ever. She said something that Amara couldn't hear. "But are you…um…planning to go back?"

At that Amara sucked in her breath and clutched her fingers into fists. "I—"

There was a loud thud. Amara swerved back quickly. Doran was lying flat on the ground. She ran toward him just as Lavinia and Kellan turned back. She crouched down beside him. "Doran! Doran!" she repeated his name, panicked. His face was drenched in sweat and screwed up in what looked like pain. He opened his mouth to respond but instead, a moan escaped his lips and he clenched his teeth. Amara looked at him in shock and desperately tried to figure out what was wrong. He was clutching the left side of his stomach with both hands. "Doran, Doran, let me look at it," she tried to say calmly, but her voice was shaking and so were her hands. She tried to move his hands away but he struggled against her. Kellan came to help Amara. He moved Doran's hands away and lifted the ripped shirt stained with red. Amara and Lavinia both gasped in horror. Doran's skin was slit open into a frightening wound. There was blood everywhere. The skin surrounding the wound was glowing with green lines spreading like vines all across his stomach.

Amara was speechless. She didn't know what to make of what she was seeing. Her heart was racing so fast and her entire body was shaking uncontrollably. She felt like she was going to vomit. She opened her mouth to try and say something but only a whimper came out. Lavinia spoke first. "What—what is this?" she said, her voice catching in her throat.

"This is—this is venom," Kellan answered, shaking his head distressfully. He pointed at the green lines spreading across Doran's side. "I think the plant got him. It was poisonous." He let out a short breath and put his hand over his face. Doran was breathing very heavily now. He was trying to open his eyes. Amara leaned closer to him. She tried to find her voice. "Doran," is all she could manage to say.

His eyes slowly opened at the sound of her voice. She stared into the brilliant green she'd grown to know so well. He licked his dry lips. Kellan hurried to give him some water. He drank slowly. Then Kellan started rummaging through his bag. Amara stayed with Doran. "This—this is because of me," she said weakly, "you saved me from that plant and it got you. This is my fault."

Doran gave his head a small shake. "No," his voice was soft. "No."

"Yes, Doran," she said a little too forcefully. "Why, why did you do that?"

"Mara," he started but then gave a grunt of pain. The green vines were all over him now and the ones around the wound were starting to turn from green to black.

Amara turned to her father, "Dad! Help him, quick!"

Kellan was still searching in his bag frantically. He glanced helplessly at Doran's wound and the spreading poison.

"Please!" she begged, starting to cry.

She felt someone grab her hand. She turned back to Doran who was trying to say something, and leaned closer to him. "Mara, it's alright. I understand," he breathed out.

"No!"

"It's too late for me, Mara."

"No! No! No! Why did you do that? Why did you have to do that? Why not just let me be, Doran? You knew it was going to get you! Why save me?" she cried.

He gave a weak smile. "I promised I'd make sure nothing bad happened to you. You have to go back to your brother. I have nothing to go back to. You have to let go now, Amara." His voice was shaky and he gasped out every word like it cost him his life. His breathing was getting slower. His face was turning from red to blue, and instead of sweating, his fingers were ice cold against Amara's hand.

"No, Doran. You're not going anywhere," Amara wept. He shut his eyes for a moment like it was difficult to keep them open. "Please," Amara was shaking her head as her tears fell over Doran's face.

Doran lifted his heavy eyelids and looked at her. Amara was once again taken aback by the shock of swirling green staring back at her. His eyes had a hint of sadness and pain in their depth but at the same time, they seemed to be at peace. Mostly, they looked sleepy. "I'm sorry," he whispered and a single tear slid from his eyes. He slowly raised his hand and gently placed his thumb on the cut on her cheek. "I'm so sorry." His hand lingered on her face a moment longer and then he dropped it to his side. He looked straight at her like it was the last time he was ever going to see her. "Mara," he breathed out her name and smiled.

"Doran, please no. Don't. Don't," she said desperately as she felt his faint heartbeats slow under her palm.

His tired eyes closed once more. "Mara," he barely moved his lips as he spoke her name this time and his voice was so low. So very low that Amara was holding her breath to make sure she caught every word. "Mara, I—" he didn't finish. A long held breath escaped his lips. His head slowly fell to the side and his cold fingers were no longer holding her hand. The ghost of a smile was still lingering on his unmoving lips.

An ugly agonized yell came out of Amara as she watched the boy with honey-colored hair go to sleep. She stood there on her knees and screamed as hot tears filled her eyes and streamed down her denying face. Her hands were stained in his blood. She was shaking and shivering madly as she stared at the boy's still figure. A gentle hand touched her shoulder. She could barely see her father through her clouding tears. Amara threw herself into him. She wept against his warm chest and let her yells and screams be muffled by his tear-soaked shirt. She let him cradle her in his strong arms. She let her tiny figure be wrapped in his. She let herself be a kid crying into her father's arms and believing all his comforting lies. She forgot all the past years. All the hurt and pain he caused. All she wanted right now was her father. To hold her and tell her it'll be alright, to shield her from all the horrors in the world, to protect her from the monsters. She held on to him so tight. She held on to him and felt him holding on to her. Holding on to her and not letting go. Holding her up, keeping her safe, soothing her with his words, trying to save her from the huge void of darkness inside of her, threatening to eat her up.

Chapter Thirty-Five

How long had it been? She didn't know. Her body was numb with pain. Her throat was burning from the screams. Her ears were bleeding from someone's deafening yells. Were they her own? She broke free from her father's embrace and tried to stand up. But she lost her balance and had to lean into one of the cold stonewalls to stand. The world was still spinning around her. Her eyes focused for a moment on the navy-haired girl standing in a corner, her red face stained with tears. Then they darted in the direction of a dark figure on the ground. It lay there completely still. Did it move? No, she imagined it. It was the wind moving the honey straws of its hair. She closed her eyes for a moment and tried to clear her mind to think straight. But she felt a heavy throbbing in her head. She could hear her own pulse beating against her skull. The memory of his faint pulse on the palm of her hand pushed itself into her consciousness but she forced it out. Her brain was so fuzzy and her body was so weak. She couldn't concentrate on anything but the strong urge to lie down on the floor and sleep. But something told her that she couldn't do that. She had to do something first.

Focus. Focus. Focus. Why was she here? There was something she so desperately needed. What was it? What was she doing in this cold and dark place? A shiver ran across her limp body and she held more tightly to the sharp rocks. She opened her eyes and stared straight ahead at the dark figure. Breathe in. Breathe out. Breathe in. Breathe out. A jerk of movement.

No. Stop. Stop this. She turned the other way. Her mind was playing tricks on her. This wasn't the time for this. She had to keep on going. She had to do something very important. She had to focus. What was it? A gasp. She turned to the corner where the blue-haired girl stood. Lavinia was staring ahead with wide eyes.

"What is it?" Kellan asked, looking up. He'd had his head down and covered with his arms.

Lavinia just stood there staring. She was moving her lips but no sound came out. Amara and Kellan both glanced at what she was looking at: the dark figure on the ground. Doran. He lay there on the ground, his head turned to one side. His face blank, eyes closed. Eyes closed and twitching. Kellan slowly approached him. He carefully put his head against Doran's chest. Slowly raising himself up, he looked at the girls with tearful eyes.

"He—he—" Kellan croaked, "he has a pulse."

An unexplainable feeling filled Amara's insides. She fell to her knees but didn't break her gaze with her father.

"It's faint," he continued, "it's very, very weak. But it's still there."

"He's alive!" Lavinia exclaimed. Something was roaring inside Amara, a feeling so strong and confusing that it burned in her stomach to her chest to every last inch of her body. But she couldn't tell if it was relief or happiness or fear or all of those together or something else entirely.

"He is," Kellan said, "but I don't know for how much longer." He lifted Doran's shirt to reveal the green vines that were now running across every last inch of him. The deep green was covering him but only the earlier lines had turned pitch black. It looked like they slowly started turning from green to black as the venom spread. "The black still hasn't reached his heart. But it's bound to eventually." Kellan examined him for a long time with a strange look on his face.

Amara couldn't bare it. They'd already thought him dead. Now they knew he was alive, but there was nothing they could do to stop him from dying. He was lying there between life and death and there was nothing they could do to save him. She had to do something. There was no way she would give up on him.

"Oh," Kellan breathed out suddenly, "oh my… How didn't I see it earlier? This is…of course."

"What?" Amara and Lavinia both said together.

"This—I've heard of this before, this kind of poison," he said, shaking his head. His hands hovered over the injured spot on Doran's stomach, and Amara noticed that red spots had started to appear all over his skin. "The symptoms look familiar. It seems similar to something I remember from my training at the Hunter corral. It's a venomous killer plant that kills slowly. The venom takes hours to spread, according to the location of the wound." He stroked his stubbly chin, deep in thought. "I think I know how to make an antidote," he said finally, not taking his eyes off of Doran.

"You can make an antidote?" Lavinia asked, a little unbelievingly, "Like, to save him? Isn't that the Healer's job?"

Kellan started rummaging through his bag again and answered her. "They teach you some stuff about that in the Hunter corral, in case someone got injured on a hunt and needed immediate medical attention. We know all the basics, and trust me we've had a lot of practice through the years. Plus, my grandmother was a Healer and she taught me a lot about making herbal medicine."

"So, you can save him?" Amara asked, she sounded out of breath.

"I hope so. I just need to gather some things, find the ingredients. And then it'll take me a while to get the medicine ready. But you can't wait here. You two have to go and get the cure for Neo."

"What?" Amara said, "go and leave Doran behind? No way."

Her father stood up and looked at her. "You can trust me, Amara. Go."

She didn't move. She wasn't really sure she could trust him actually.

"Amara…" He stood closer to her and placed his hands on her shoulders. She had to stop herself from pulling away at first. He looked at her for a long moment before talking again.

"You're not the little girl I left back home anymore, are you? You've grown. You've grown so much and I'm sorry I wasn't there to see it. I'm sorry if I've forced you to abandon your childhood and grow up so fast. I'm sorry I left. I'm so sorry for everything I put you through, my darling." He was going to say something but then stopped himself. "I know that my promises are probably empty words to you, and it's hard for you to trust me. But I am asking you to trust me now. You can go, get the cure for your brother. And when you come back, I'll be right here. I will do my very best to save your friend, honey. I won't let you down. I believe in you, love. I trust you can do this. And please, no matter what, remember that I love you." He pulled her into a tight hug. They pulled out of the hug but Kellan kept his hands on her shoulders for a moment longer before forcing them down. Amara looked into her father's loving eyes. She really had to keep going, and truly hoped she could trust him. She glanced at Doran. Then stood there for a minute, trying to will herself into believing her father. She nodded once then hesitated for a moment, wanting to tell him something before leaving. But instead of doing that, she just turned and started walking away.

Chapter Thirty-Six

Amara and Lavinia walked toward the distant door. "Do you think they're doing okay back home?" Amara asked. She pointed her flashlight around, checking for any poisonous plants. There weren't any in sight.

"They've still got time," Lavinia said, "and the Healers will take good care of them 'til we come back. Well, that's if—"

"We'll make it back home," Amara said with a determined look on her face. "We will."

Lavinia nodded. She glanced at Amara. "You're not as bad as I thought you were." She paused for a little. "It was easier to be a total jerk to you if I convinced myself that you were a bad person, you know? But you're not that bad."

Amara smiled at her. "Thank you, I guess? You're not that awful yourself, when you're not trying to kill me or whatever."

Lavinia gave a short laugh. "Thanks."

They stood before the door. Now that they saw it up close, it wasn't exactly a door. More like an opening carved in the stonewalls. The light inside was so blinding that they couldn't see past it.

"Should we go in?" Lavinia asked.

"There's no other way."

They looked at each other one last time before stepping into the yellow curtain of light. Amara felt a tingling go through her entire body. She had to close her eyes because the light around her was so blinding. Then there was silence. Complete silence. No dripping water. No echoing footsteps, nothing. Amara opened her eyes and saw darkness. Pitch black darkness like she's never seen before. There was not the tiniest bit of light. It was so dark that she had to blink more than once to make sure her eyes weren't closed.

Amara quickly reached for the switch on her flashlight. After clicking on it more than ten times she realized that it wasn't working. Maybe the battery was dead. A shudder washed over her body. She kept turning around as if to check that there wasn't anything behind her, not that she would see it. Her hands were shaking uncontrollably as she glanced around her, unable to see a thing. Her breathes were shallow and her heartbeats fast. She was sweating but trembling. All she was able to think about was how very dark it was. The blackness was all around her. It was wrapping its colorless arms around her and trapping her in her worst nightmare. She felt so lost and alone. She was in the middle of nowhere. She was a wandering soul detached from her body. She wasn't sure she even existed anymore. What was real, what was not?

Amara spun and spun around herself trying to find a way out. She had to go out. She had to escape. She had to leave this place, this empty place. She had to leave the dark before she turned into nothing. She couldn't breathe. Tears were choking her and there wasn't enough oxygen, or she forgot how to take it from the air. She felt powerless. She felt so helpless against this unbearable blackness. Amara shut her eyes so tight and wrapped her arms around herself, rocking back and forth. Please, please, please make this end, she begged to no one. But nothing happened.

She was still in the dark, all alone, so miserably alone. Her hand went up to her chest, which was tightening with fear. A cold metal touched her fingers. She pulled the small locket out of her shirt. She couldn't see it of course, but she had memorized the shape of it from the countless of nights she had spent staring at it in her tiny hands. Even in the dark, she could still imagine the round golden pendant, gone rusty around the edges. The beautiful rose carved into it delicately. Amara opened the locket. She imagined the happy faces of her parents and brother staring back at her. Her mother's gentle words played again in her head. *As long as you have this, you'll know I'll always be with you.* She wasn't alone, she wasn't alone. She tried to convince herself that. She stood up – ignoring her shaky legs – and shouted.

"Lavinia!"

"Amara," she heard Lavinia's voice.

Chapter Thirty-Seven

Somehow, although it was still dark, she could see some light coming from somewhere. But she still couldn't distinguish where they were or what was around her.

"Lavinia?" she called again, and heard the panic in her voice. She saw Lavinia's figure standing a few feet in front of her but still couldn't see her clearly.

"Are you afraid of the dark?" Lavinia asked. Her voice was clearer this time. There was a slight hint of mockery in her tone.

"I—I—" Amara started, she was a little out of breath.

"I can't believe it!" Lavinia laughed. "You're afraid of the dark?" Amara was shocked to hear her talk like that again. "How are you supposed to save your little brother if you're afraid of something so silly like darkness?" There was definitely a clear sign of mockery in her voice this time. Amara stayed quiet.

"What else are you afraid of? I'm sure you're terrified of a thousand other ridiculous things, aren't you?" Lavinia's voice was full of pleasure now. "Of course you are. You're nothing but a fourteen-year-old girl that misses her mommy and is waiting for her daddy to come back home and save the day. You couldn't even take care of your little brother! You had one simple job and that was to look after him. Guess what? You failed!"

Amara's heart fell into her stomach. What was this? Why was she talking this way?

"Surprise, surprise. You can't do anything right, can you? You couldn't even find yourself a stupid corral. You don't fit anywhere. You're an outcast, a mistake, a burden on our society. Why do you think they let you work all around in the other corrals? Because they feel sorry for you, of course. Poor little orphan Amara; she doesn't have any parents, doesn't have any money, and doesn't have a corral."

Hot tears were welling in Amara's eyes as she heard the truth spoken aloud for the first time. All her fears and unspoken concerns were being pulled out of her mind and voiced out loud.

"Even your friend feels sorry for you. That's the only reason she even talks to you. You think she likes you? Of course she doesn't, no one does. That's why your dad left. He couldn't stand to be burdened with you and your problems any longer."

Amara was beginning to feel dizzy somehow. Her heart was still racing so fast. The words she was hearing were thrashing against her head. *You couldn't even take care of your little brother. You don't fit anywhere. You think she likes you? Of course she doesn't, no one does. That's why your dad left. He couldn't stand to be burdened with you and your problems any longer.*

But…

No matter what, remember that I love you.

Her father had said that with his eyes brimming with affection. She remembered Neo's face when she picked him up from school, how he ran to her with a huge smile on his face and hugged her tight. She remembered Elianah, how they lay down together and laughed so hard at the amazing memories they had shared together. She remembered Healer Evetta and her Aunt Kaila and her mother.

"No," she said to Lavinia. Her voice was hurt, but somehow brave. "That's not true. None of it is true."

She waited for Lavinia to respond but something happened. A white mist filled the air around them. It blocked out everything and Amara couldn't see anything except for the white fog. Then, as she squinted against the mist, she caught sight of a doorway. A different doorway than the one they had entered from. It seemed to be an entrance to a room. She walked closer. She could see inside that room now. Strangely, it looked very much like one of the hospital rooms back in Kumilaka. It also had a bed just like the ones at the hospital. On this bed lay a little boy with spikes of green hair.

Chapter Thirty-Eight

Amara stumbled as she walked towards her brother. She was inside the hospital room, back home in Kumilaka. Neo was lying in the big bed in front of her. She looked at his beautiful face. It was very pale. His eyes were closed. As she walked closer, she noticed the pitch-black markings etched on his skin like fresh ink. They enveloped every last inch of his body and had already claimed his life as theirs.

The walls were caving in on her. The ceiling was cracking. The ground was shaking. Her entire world was collapsing. Her heart, instead of beating so fast, had stopped beating entirely. She was swaying, falling. She lay there on the ground with no memory of how she got there. Tears didn't fall. Screams never came. She was completely paralyzed. Both her heart and mind were still. The pain was so overwhelming that she couldn't feel a thing. Everything was for nothing. It was all over. There wasn't any point to anything anymore. It was all gone. Giving up was the only option now. There was no point in trying. No point in living. She stayed there, waiting for the world to turn black, waiting to be buried by the rubble, waiting to be no more.

As she stared into nothingness, a face flashed before her. A mess of dirty blond hair, a pair of lime green eyes, a smile. Doran still needed her. Zuri still needed her. A countless number of children in Kumilaka still needed her. Maybe this wasn't real. Maybe Neo still needed her. She wouldn't know if she lay here on the ground and gave up. Her heart was still beating. She was still breathing. No matter what, she couldn't give up. Not yet.

Amara started to get up. But before she could even glance back at the boy on the bed, the world started to change again.

The white mist was back. It clouded her vision. Before it faded away, Amara caught the sweet scent of a thousand flowers. Sure enough, as the white began to fade away; she was stunned to see an endless field of the most beautiful and colorful flowers she had ever laid her eyes upon. Colors were splattered everywhere, the soft purple of lilac, the bright yellow of daffodils, the vibrant pink of lilies, and the countless shades of blue all scattered around. Amara couldn't begin to count how many colors she saw and she wouldn't dream to know half of the types of flowers there. The sight was unbelievably gorgeous. There was a soft breeze and it tickled the leaves and petals to move ever so slightly in a graceful dance. The sky above was so clear and so brilliantly blue and it calmly looked over the endless sea of beauty. Filling the air was the heavenly fragrance of flowers and wet grass. The blossoms looked expectantly toward the sky and were graciously bathed by the warm glow of the yellow sun.

In this quiet meadow, between the thick green grass, and under the infinite blue of the sky, Amara felt a strange sense of peacefulness for the first time in forever. She allowed herself to take in a deep breath of fresh air and let it out slowly. She listened closely to the steady beating of her heart, egging her on and pushing her forward. She took a step forward. She didn't know where she was going. She just had this feeling. She walked through the field of flowers. She walked and walked. She saw all the colors imaginable and all the shades possible, until she reached a clearing where a bunch of white flowers were growing. She stopped. The roses were so supremely white, so pure with it that they were practically glowing. Amara had never seen roses so delicate and elegant before. Every single one of these roses looked perfectly angelic. She leaned down and reached to pick one up. As she pulled it up, she felt a sharp prick of one of the thorns on its stem.

"Ouch!" she licked her finger and tasted something metallic, the drop of her blood.

She looked at the rose in her other hand. The weirdest thing was happening. The white petals of the rose were slowly transforming into another color. In seconds, they had turned from the brilliant white they were to the deepest shade of red.

"I had a feeling it might be you."

Chapter Thirty-Nine

Amara startled at the sound. She spun around quickly, holding up her hands in defense. There was a strange man standing a short distance away. He was wearing an old cloak. When he lifted up his head to look at her, she was shocked to realize that he was the same old man that gave them the directions to the mountains. He had a thick white beard and hair. His eyes were a gleaming black. He was short, or more like tall and with a stooped posture. The man was leaning on a wooden cane and smiling knowingly at Amara.

"What...?" she couldn't even bring herself to form a question. She stood there staring at him, still holding her arms up in the air.

The man laughed softly. "Don't worry, my dear child," he said gently, "I am not here to hurt you. I simply live here in these very mountains."

"You—you live here?" she asked, unconvinced.

"Yes, I do. These mountains are my home." He gestured at his surroundings. "Of course, I do move around every now and then and visit some other places when needed. Like when you saw me at the village not very long ago."

"What did you mean just now; when you said you had a feeling it was me?"

"I have some instinctive feelings occasionally and when I saw you, something told me that you'll be the one."

"The one? The one to what?"

"The one to earn the trust of the mountains, of course. The one to succeed in passing. The Savior."

"What? What are you talking about?" Amara was beginning to feel weirded out.

"I have already told you," he said patiently, "many have tried to pass. But none have succeeded. The belief is that there will only be one to succeed. Clearly, that one is you."

"What do you mean me? Pass what?" Amara really wished he would stop talking in gibberish already and get to the point.

He gave a small smile. "You have passed the test. You have earned the trust of the mountains. Therefore, you may take from them what you please. You are here for something, aren't you?"

"I'm here for—for the cure. I heard that the cure for the Touch is in the Mountains of Emberose but I…" she trailed off.

"Exactly, you are here for something. You are not the first one to come for it, of course. There were many before you. But you are the first one to succeed when all the others have failed, because you are not here in search of fame or glory, love or riches. And because *you* are the one meant to retrieve the cure you are looking for. You are The Savior."

"What do you mean succeed? I haven't succeeded. And who's this savior you keep talking about?"

The old man chuckled. "Yes, you have, my darling. And the savior is you, of course."

When he saw the still confused look on Amara's face he continued.

"What do you think the marking on your forehead means then?"

"I don't know what it means. No one does. I don't have a known corral like everyone else in Kumilaka does."

"That's because there is only one of you. There is only one Savior of your land and that is you. Your marking is one of a kind, my dear. It is like no other because there is only one person who can be granted such a role. That person is you. You are The Savior of your land."

"What does that even mean? I'm the savior? What exactly does that make me?"

"As I understand, your land has been touched by a great tragedy. It is a tragedy that has been present amongst your people for a very long time. They have tried to save their loved ones from it but failed. They have since then just let it happen because there was nothing else they could do. But now, a soul most brave and honorable has emerged, a soul worthy of saving millions of lives. And that is you. You are The Savior. You are the only one capable of saving all those souls and bringing peace to your land. You are the only one who has the power to bring back the cure that has long been awaited by your people. The cure you hold in your very hands."

Amara looked down at her hands and saw the beautiful rose with blood red petals. She raised it to the old man with a questioning look in her eyes.

"Yes," he said, "that is the cure you are looking for."

CHAPTER FORTY

The rose was rich in color. It looked as if at any moment blood would drip from its shivering petals. Amara turned it between her fingers. It was almost impossible to believe. What would even make her believe a word this strange man said? He was talking nonsense just like the first time they saw him, except he wasn't talking nonsense back then. He did give them the right directions to the mountains, and apparently he knew a lot about her home, the Touch, and the cure. Or did he? How could she know for sure? These were all theories and assumptions. None of this was for sure. Maybe he was just playing with her head and filling it with lies and fairytales. Maybe there wasn't even a cure out here in the first place. She never knew there was for sure. But she still came. She still hung to the tiniest sliver of hope she could find and sought to make it true. Why? She didn't know. But perhaps the same reason that led her to venture beyond the safety of her home and cross the ocean to find a mythical cure is what's allowing her to believe this man and his impossible truths.

"Let's say I believe you," Amara studied the old man carefully. "I'm not saying that I do. But let's imagine for a moment that what you're saying is true and what I'm holding in my hands is the cure I'm looking for. It can't be that easy, right? You said I succeeded. How did I succeed? I didn't even do anything. I just found it. What is this test you're talking about? The test I passed?"

The old man smiled knowingly. He stroked his white beard and started talking. "You most certainly did do something. You didn't just find it. The mountains willingly presented it to you, after they tested you. They tested your strength, your will, and determination. They tested your bravery, your selflessness, and your deep desire to help others. But most importantly, they tested your faith. Your faith in other people, your faith in yourself, and your unquestionable faith in what you believe in. Your strong and unwavering will to hold on to something that you don't even know exists. You weren't given any proof or guarantees that what you're looking for is actually there. All you had was the strength of your heart and the flame of hope burning deep in your soul. And sometimes, that's all you need."

Amara was a little stunned by what she was hearing. But it was as if someone was holding her hand and telling her that all of it wasn't for nothing. That it actually mattered. "But how did—when was I tested?"

"You were tested every step of the way, of course," he said, raising his eyebrows, "your final test was what you encountered when you walked into the doorway. You had to face your biggest fears. Fear of the dark. Fear of the truth. Fear of loss."

The darkness flashed in her mind, Lavinia and her hurtful words, Neo and the black on his skin.

"So, all that…it wasn't real?"

"They were simple illusions. Your own worries and fears displayed in front of you in disguise."

"And I what? Beat my fears?"

"In a way, perhaps. You were still afraid of the dark, of course. But the point was not to conquer your fear, it was to have the strength to keep moving on despite it, to not let it control you and render you of your power. And you didn't. Then you heard the truths you've been trying to hide inside yourself all those years. But you realized that they weren't the truth after all. They were lies you made up yourself. They were your own uncertainties and doubts that you forced your own eyes to see reflected on other people's faces when they weren't there at all.

"Lastly, you were faced with your biggest fear, the fear that has repeated itself in your past many times. You were afraid for it to happen again. You were still afraid of the ones that have already happened. But most of all, you were afraid that they were your fault. But you had to admit to yourself that the losses that you faced in the past and might face in the future are not because of you. They are not your fault nor will they ever be. And even though they will hurt a lot and cause you unbearable pain, you must find within yourself the power and the courage to keep going and not give up. You must remember that there are still people in your life that love and need you, people who care about you. And the people that you lost, they are still here with you, even when it is hard to see sometimes. You still have their love and it gives you the power you need to move on. But you also have to move on for you."

Amara nodded. His gentle words were somehow reassuring.

"Now, my dear, you have proven yourself worthy. You have proven yourself as The Savior of your people. You, my child, are their flame of hope. Hope for a better future, one where there is less pain. Now go. Take the cure back to them. Give them what they have long awaited and free them of this great fear they have struggled with endlessly. Take them." He gestured toward the roses. "They are a gift from the Mountains of Emberose to The Savior."

She looked back at the white roses. There was an empty basket on the floor beside them that she could have sworn was not there before. Amara leaned down again. She dug up the flowers with their roots and placed them carefully into the basket, covering them again with soil. Then she got up and turned to thank the old man. But he was gone. She looked around the field but couldn't see him anywhere.

"Thank you," Amara said. The words were a whisper into the air, filled with gratitude.

The white mist filled her surroundings once more and the aroma of the flowers faded away as she felt her feet hit the hard floor of the cave.

Chapter Forty-One

She was back in front of the doorway. Except now it looked dark inside. She blinked and it miraculously disappeared. Nothing was left except for the solid wall of the cave, standing still as if it had always been there. The flashlight was lying on the floor. She picked it up and tried it. It worked.

"Amara?"

Lavinia hurried toward her. "Where were you? When we walked inside I—I don't know what happened I couldn't get through and you were gone and—"

"I'm alright," Amara said, "it's all good. I got the cure." She raised the basket of flowers in her hands.

"You what?" Lavinia was incredulous. She started asking a million questions at once.

"I'll explain everything later, I promise. But right now, we have to get back. We don't know how much time we've got left."

Lavinia was about to argue but then changed her mind. They turned back to find Kellan and Doran.

When they found their way back, Kellan practically jumped up at the sight of them. As Amara ran toward them, she could see his eyes filled with so many different emotions that she couldn't tell apart.

"We found it! We got it!" they yelled.

A mixture of relief and excitement washed over his face. Then he crouched down again, focusing on the things in front of him. He was concentrating on adding very precise amounts of things and then stirring them in what looked like a very professional and impressive way. It looked as though he had gathered some ingredients from some place and used some of the stuff they had packed. He was mixing them inside a wooden bowl.

"How's it going with the antidote?" Lavinia asked tentatively.

"Almost done with it," Kellan muttered, "I just need to…" he crumpled something up and added it to the mixture and then proceeded in doing other things Amara didn't understand. She noticed one of the venomous plants on the floor and jumped back at the sight of it. But she quickly realized it was dead and motionless.

Kellan caught her staring at it. "I needed it for the antidote. It's quite ironic, but you need parts of the poisoner to cure the poisoned."

As he continued to work, Amara leaned down to check up on Doran. Kellan had covered him with his own jacket and coat and he sat there now with only his shirt, the sleeves pulled up as he quickly worked on the medicine. Doran's face was as pale as she'd ever seen it. He looked somehow transparent, as if he were a ghost. His slightly parted lips were a bluish purple. His body was so still but Amara could feel him shuddering under the layers of clothes he was covered with. She thanked her father silently. Carefully, she lifted the clothes up to check on his wound. It was covered in bandages; Kellan must have done this to keep it from getting infected. But the skin surrounding it looked absolutely awful. She could see that the black was almost covering his entire body now. It was glowing against his pale skin and spreading on the inside, traveling through his veins. She quickly covered him up again and flinched when her hand brushed his ice-cold skin. She looked at his motionless face with anguish. What she would give to see him open his lime green eyes again. What she would give to see one of his never-ending smiles plastered on his childish face one more time.

"I think it's ready," Kellan breathed out and wiped the sweat on his forehead with his sleeve. He hurried toward them with a wooden bowl of what looked like porridge, only it had a nasty and strange color, a mix of green and brown with chunks of red and black. "This is sort of a complicated one to make. But I did have a lot of practice with it. They used to call me the Healer of the pack. So, let's cross our fingers that it will work." Kellan looked a little nervous, but also had a sort of proud look on his face. Lavinia crouched down as well and lifted Doran's head up. Kellan started feeding him the medicine, forcing him to swallow it while he lay there unconscious. And all Amara could do was watch. Watch and hope and beg and beg that this will work. She dug her fingernails into the palms of her hands and made fists so tight that her knuckles turned white. *Please, please, please make this work*, she begged in her head. Doran's body was still unstirring in Lavinia's arms, his face remained emotionless. Amara's breaths were coming out faster. "This had to work. He had to wake up. He had to.

Doran body gave a jerk, then another one. He gasped loudly. Something was happening to him. He suddenly started shaking and breathing so hard and fast. Amara noticed the sweat breaking from his forehead. His face had turned a bright shade of red as if he had a fever. His chest was heaving and he was gasping, trying to catch his breath. Amara hurried to move the heavy layers of clothing away from him. She felt the heat rising from his body. How crazy was it that only a moment ago he was a freezing corpse and now he was practically on fire. She took a look at the bandaged wound on his side. The bandages were dirty and bloody now. The black lines around them were still there, but they were definitely lighter than they were before. Their color was slowly fading away. She looked at his face for the hundredth time. His eyes were still closed, but not in the helpless way they were before. They were shut tight as Doran started letting out grunts and sighs of pain.

"I think it's working!" Kellan said exasperatedly.

"I think it is!" Lavinia said. There was a joy in her voice that Amara had never quite heard there before.

Amara could almost cry from happiness herself, but not yet. She had to see his eyes, open and awake.

"I'll change his bandages again," Kellan hurried to work.

By the time Doran's bandages were freshly replaced, his body had calmed down a bit and his breaths were almost steady. Kellan had just offered to carry him so they could head back to the village when his eyes fluttered. The green was as beautiful as ever. An overwhelming sense of joy and relief washed over Amara. She put her hands on her mouth to prevent the sob from escaping, but she still dropped to her knees. Doran's blurry eyes focused on her.

"Mara," he said hoarsely, giving her a weak smile.

She then broke into tears. But for the first time in a very long time, they were happy tears.

Chapter Forty-Two

They were back at that inn where Amara's father had been staying. They had come to gather essentials for the long journey back home and decided to spend the rest of the night there because it will be easier to set sail in the morning, and Doran still needed to rest. Amara and Lavinia took a room to themselves and Doran was staying with Kellan.

"Can you believe we actually did it?" Lavinia said in a whisper. Amara and Lavinia were both lying in bed now. "I mean, you actually did it. You're the one who found the cure."

"You know that's not true," Amara said, "I could never have even gotten there without you guys. I mean, how on earth would I have sailed a boat in the middle of the ocean and fought through a storm? Or stabbed a huge sea monster in the eye? I couldn't have done any of this without you. We did it together."

"Yeah," Lavinia said between a huge yawn, "we did, didn't we? And tomorrow, we're going back home." Amara could hear the sleepy smile in her voice. A few minutes of silence later, Lavinia's breathes were slow and heavy, which meant she had drifted away to sleep. Something that Amara had a feeling she wouldn't be able to do right now. There was something still bugging her. She quietly got out of bed and slid out the bedroom door, which she closed behind her carefully. Just as she walked out, she found her father coming up the stairs. He saw her too and stopped in his tracks.

"Hey," he said.

"Hey."

"I was going to get a drink and clear my head before bed," he said, pointing down the stairs. "I changed my mind."

Amara nodded. She turned around to go back to her room.

"No, wait, don't leave because of me. I was just going back inside to check on Doran. You can—"

"I wasn't leaving because of you," Amara's voice came out a little cold.

"Oh, okay then."

She turned around again.

"Wait," Kellan said again, "can we talk?"

"Talk?" she repeated.

"Yes. Please?"

She sighed, "Fine."

They walked to a quiet corner. They stood there for a moment, staring at each other. Or more like avoiding staring at each other.

"Thank you," Amara said finally, "for saving Doran." He had done as he promised. She came back and found him there. He had saved Doran. That meant to her more than she could tell him. But that didn't mean she wasn't still mad at him.

"You shouldn't thank me," Kellan said firmly. He closed his eyes and took in a long and deep breath then let it out. "Amara, I'm sorry. I know I might have already said that but... I want you to know that I am. I am so very deeply sorry for what I put you and your little brother through." She flinched slightly at his mention of Neo. "I want you to know that leaving was the biggest regret of my life, and I know that your heart is filled with so much anger toward me for what I've done, and I deserve every bit of it. But I'm sorry." He stopped talking and took a step closer to her. Very slowly, he moved his hands and held her face in them. She tensed a little at his touch. He stroked her red hair and a couple of tears slid down his face.

"You have become so much like your mother, Amara. I don't know what she was going to say if she knew what I've done to you beautiful kids. I made a mistake, a huge and unforgivable mistake. I neither deserve your love nor sympathy, Amara. I don't deserve your forgiveness. All I ask of you is to remember. Please remember that I love you more than I can ever tell you. Maybe that same love led to the fear that made me leave. But I promise you now that I won't ever leave you again." Her heart trembled at these words.

"You might still believe that my promises are pointless words, and you have every right to, because they might have been that way once. But my regret is swallowing me whole, Amara. That's why I never got the nerve to return after all those years. I couldn't face you. I couldn't face the mistakes I've done. So I just stayed away. I stayed away, drunken in my sorrow and regret. That was so very wrong of me. I left you guys when you needed me the most. I failed you," his voice cracked. "But I vow to you now that I will do everything in my power to fix my mistakes. I will take care of you and your brother and protect you from anything that might hurt you. And from now on, I will never ever allow anything in the world to drive me away." His lips trembled as he forced out the words with a look of desperate determination that Amara had never seen in his eyes before. "I promise you, my love. I promise you, I will, if you let me. I want to come back home with you. I want to come home. Will you please let me?"

Amara closed her eyes and let the tears slide down. This was what she always wanted, for her father to come home. But his betrayal has filled her with pain and anger that she couldn't just erase that simply. She couldn't forgive him that easily. Not yet. She couldn't hand him back her trust. He had to earn it back. So maybe he deserved a chance to do just that. She opened her eyes and looked at their reflection on her father's weary face. They were full of promises. Promises she hoped with all her heart that he would stay true to. And so she nodded.

Chapter Forty-Three

Before going to bed, Amara went in to check on Doran. He was standing near the bed with his shoes on his feet, no doubt totally ignoring Kellan's instructions to stay in bed and rest. Amara noticed he was looking at something he held in his hands, it looked like a tattered piece of paper. As soon as he realized Amara had walked in, he shoved it into his bag and jumped onto his bed to act as if he were there the whole time. Amara saw how his fingers briefly traveled to the left side of his stomach and rubbed the spot lightly.

"Hi," he smiled as he looked at her.

"Hello," she said and went to sit on the chair across from him. She studied him. His face was still somewhat pale, and he looked a little feverish. He was good at disguising it, but Amara could still tell that he was in pain from the way he sat stiffly on the bed and clutched the sheets tightly. "How are you feeling?" she asked.

"Amazing, considering I just came back from the dead." Doran grinned.

"You did not come back from the dead," Amara rolled her eyes.

"Oh, I so did, according to Lavinia at least. She also said you cried a river for me," he teased.

"Oh, shut up," she threw a cushion at him but he ducked and it hit the wall. "Mind you, her face wasn't that dry either."

"Wow, looks like I have a lot of admirers."

"If you dare rub that in our faces in the future, you just might find yourself dead again."

He laughed, but then his face turned into a frown.

"What's wrong?"

"I have to tell you something."

"What?"

He looked at Amara hesitantly.

"What is it? Tell me, I won't bite your head off."

"I'm not going back home with you guys."

"What?" Amara wasn't expecting him to say that.

"I'm not going back to Kumilaka."

"What do you mean you're not going back? It's your home!"

He was quiet for a moment before saying, "I've never felt at home there, not really," he was staring at the bed and playing with one of the strings sticking out of the blanket on it, twisting it around his finger. "It's like I told you, I don't have anything to go back to. My uncle never wanted me to live with him in the first place. All I am to him is his punching bag." He laughed but once again Amara heard that hint of bitterness in his voice. "And I've always felt like Kumilaka, as great as it is, wasn't enough for me.

"Ever since I was a kid, I dreamed of going on an adventure. And this adventure we just had was an amazing one, and it was all thanks to you." He smiled at her and she could see the little boy in his eyes again. "But I'm not ready to go home. I don't want to settle for whatever life I can make for myself back there. I mean, there's a whole world out there, and I want to see it.

"I love my role as a Messenger, I really do. But I've always felt like I was meant for more, you know? Like there were bigger messages for me to deliver, and I want to find out what they are. If I'm being honest with myself, I guess the moment I rode on that boat with you guys and we sailed away, I never meant to go back. I don't want to."

Amara gave him a sad smile. "Don't worry, I get it. And I do believe you're meant to do big things, Doran. I mean look at what you helped do on this adventure you came on. We found the cure! I bet that'll be the biggest message Kumilaka would be receiving in history. And they'll always know it was thanks to you."

His eyes sparkled at her words, but he didn't let his smile betray him. "So, you're not mad?"

"I'm not, I promise."
He then smiled broadly.

Chapter Forty-Four

They got up at sunrise. Lavinia was getting the boat ready to sail. Amara, Doran, and Kellan were packing everything they'll need into it. Amara took the basket of roses into her cabin. They were still as fresh and vibrant as they were before she'd picked them up from the meadow. But she still made sure to carefully place them by the tiny round window in the cabin, and sprayed the wet soil with a little more water. They were finally ready to go.

"I talked to Agatha and she said she was glad to have me stay with her for a while," Doran told Amara as they stood on the rocky shore. "I actually found a guy that said he'll consider letting me come along on their ship if I helped the crew with work, I'll go and see where the ocean takes me."

She smiled at his enthusiasm. She realized then that his smiles actually were contagious. "You'll do great on all the adventures you'll go on."

"I hope so—" he paused, "I never thanked you."

"Thanked me?"

"You saved my life."

"No, I didn't. My dad did."

"Well he's your dad, so it was because of you he was there. Also," he said in a lower tone, "I could feel you cheering me on. Not giving up on me. I was going to give up on myself really. But the whole time, I could see your face somewhere in the distance, and so I forced myself to hold on just a little longer. And then I woke up, and there you were, still not giving up hope for me."

Amara was quiet. She stared at Doran, his green eyes full of truth and wonder. His words warmed her heart and started a tingling feeling in her stomach. She cleared her throat and forced her own words out. "Well, you saved mine first."

"Then we're even." He laughed.

"I guess we are."

"But thank you."

"No." She shook her head. "Thank you for helping me do this. It would've been impossible without you."

"Then I'm glad I came," he said smugly. She laughed.

The waves were smashing loudly against the rocks and splattering water on their faces.

"I'm proud of you, Mara. I knew you could do it."

She smiled. "I know you can do it too. Just be careful, okay?"

He was going to say something but then Lavinia shouted from the boat.

"If you two love birds are done here, we have to go!"

"Go on, they're waiting for you," Doran told her. Amara got on the boat and Doran stood on the shore to see them off. Kellan road last and gave Doran one of those guy hugs and Doran hugged him back. Then he squeezed his shoulder and said something before getting on.

"Hey, clown-face," Lavinia called to Doran, "see you later."

"You sure will," Doran smiled at her. "You haven't seen the last of me or my pickle eyes just yet."

She laughed.

"Have a safe trip," he waved to them.

"And you have an amazing trip yourself," Amara called to him, "But don't forget us, okay?"

"There's no way!" he shouted back as the crashing of the waves grew louder. He smiled his widest smile and waved to them as the boat sailed away. The rising sun cast a magical glow on his golden hair. As the boat sailed farther his figure became smaller, until he became a tiny speck in the distance, a black dot in the beautiful orange sky.

Amara stared at the early morning sky and the wild waves that made up this restless ocean. And she marveled at the wonder of it all, the vastness of this universe, the greatness of everything in it. She took it all in and let the feeling that it gave her simmer inside her soul. The possibilities it all promised. How could anything be impossible? How could anything be out of reach? When all this existed? She felt a deep peacefulness. She felt an undeniable and untouchable sense of hope.

Epilogue

Their small house was full. The kitchen table was crowded with food and sweets. Light was creeping in through the windows as the curtains hung open. The afternoon sun was casting glorious beams of light on the freshly cleaned floors. Amara glanced out of the window to her right – the one that had been fixed three years ago and looked brand new – and saw everyone outside on the yard. Grown-ups were crowding around the table and chatting, girls were sitting around in groups gossiping and laughing, kids were playing, and toddlers were running around. Amara picked up the giant box sitting at the middle of the table – the one that Baker Rosemarie brought earlier today – and walked out of her house to the gathering outside. On one side of the garden were a bunch of beautiful pearly white flowers that bloomed graciously in the direction of the sun. The Savior roses had been planted all over Kumilaka years ago and now grew regularly across the land. The Morbus Touch was still in Kumilaka, but now it could be cured and innocent lives could be saved. Amara had to be the one to give the cure to the children who'd been touched, after the Healers prepared the medicine using the Savior roses; it was her role as the Savior of the land. A new marking had been added to the Book of Markings in Kumilaka, Amara's marking.

She reached the table where all the parents stood.

"Here's my little girl," her dad squeezed her into a hug and she held out the box with both hands so it didn't get squished in the hug.

"Hey, hey, hey," a pretty woman with curls of pink hair took the box from her and placed it carefully on the table. It was Carer Nadine, the kind lady that worked in the Children's

Home. Well, now she was much more than that. She was Amara's mother and her father's wife. They had met when he came back to Kumilaka and married a year and a half ago. "Be careful with my baby's cake," she said to Kellan, "thank you, honey," she said to Amara and gave her a kiss her on the head. "Now go call everyone so we can cut the cake!"

Amara walked away and started gathering everyone. She spotted Elianah, Jovie, Lavinia, and Coreen all standing together and chattering.

"Mara, where did you go?" Elianah said as soon as she saw her. "Did you hear Jovie's story from work?" she said through laughter.

"You mean the one about mischievous children and missing crayons?" Amara asked.

Jovie laughed.

"I don't understand how you could possibly handle a class full of those crazy munchkins every day," Amara said, laughing too. Jovie was an Educator.

"At least," Coreen started, "she doesn't have to convince them to brush their teeth every morning and night, and go to bed on time, and eat their meals and—"

"We get it," Jovie cut her off. "Speaking of crazy munchkins, I think we better gather them up because it looks like they're cutting the cake up soon."

"Oh goodness, not again!" Elianah hurried toward what looked like a boy being held in a headlock by a small, but apparently very strong, girl.

Lavinia ran after her, "Zuri, how many times do we have to talk about this?!" she called to the small girl, "put that boy down, now!"

"I think they can handle that one on their own," Jovie said, attempting to keep a straight face but failing. She walked toward the running kids and called out to them in her authoritative voice. They all scampered away toward the long table in excitement, almost all of them. Jovie grabbed her brother Sev, whose silver hair had grown into a giant afro, from the ear and pulled him toward the others.

"Ouch ouch ouch ouch," he whimpered like a kid, "I was *coming.*"

Someone giggled from behind them. Amara turned around and saw her brother Neo. His grass green hair spiked out of his head in all directions and he grinned his childish grin as his chestnut eyes wrinkled on the edges. On his forehead sat a handsome marking, one that said he was a Crafter. Neo was holding a bowl of pudding and he shoved the last spoonful of it into his mouth, which was covered in chocolate, like a kid's.

"Come on," Amara wiped his face with her sleeve and he wrinkled his nose, annoyed. Then she threw her arm over his shoulder as they walked after the others. "Time for cake."

"My favorite words," he said.

They all sat around the long table. On the head of the table were Amara, Neo, their father, his wife, and a tiny baby toddler with peels of lemon as hair. The cake sat in front of them. It was a big chocolate cake. Neat spongy layers over one another all decorated with fluffy white frosting and topped off with fresh blueberries and raspberries. On the top face of the cake – written in frosting with pretty letters – it said: *"HAPPY 1st BIRTHDAY DO"* (Short for Doran, the boy who had saved both Kellan and his daughter's lives). Amara closed her eyes for a second and took in the delightful scent filling the air. The cake smelled like sheer chocolaty joy. Her mouth watered as she imagined the rich and moist sweetness melting in her mouth when she'd take a bite. It seemed that she wasn't the only one who'd noticed the delicious smell though, little Doran was fighting to free himself from his mother's arms to get a hold of his cake. His pretty, lemon yellow curls were bouncing on his head as his mom tried to hold him out of the way until Kellan cut the cake.

After everyone got a piece of cake, and they all started eating, one of Carer Nadine's friends came to take a picture of them. That picture would later hang in the living room of that small house at the edge of the woods for years to come. In the picture, Nadine – her pink hair falling onto her face – lovingly held Amara's baby brother with curls of lemon on his head and a face stained with chocolate as she leaned happily into Kellan's shoulders. Her father's head hung back as he laughed joyously, his hands were on both his children's shoulders. Neo stood beside Amara and smiled his big, happy smile, causing the edges of his eyes to crinkle under the mess of green hair. Amara stood in the middle and smiled happily as she looked at everyone, her flaming red hair was vibrant as always and the light breeze carried it up slightly. Her bangs were no longer covering her forehead, where lay a beautiful marking etched into her skin, the marking of a Savior.

THE END